MOTHER WEST WIND'S NEIGHBORS

New Illustrated Edition

MOTHER
WEST WIND'S
NEIGHBORS

New Illustrated Edition

by

THORNTON W. BURGESS

With Illustrations by Harrison Cady

Foreword by Charles E. Roth
of the Massachusetts Audubon Society

LITTLE, BROWN AND COMPANY
BOSTON • NEW YORK • TORONTO • LONDON

Republished in 1985
10 9 8 7 6

Library of Congress Cataloging in Publication Data

Burgess, Thornton W. (Thornton Waldo), 1874–1965.
  Mother west wind's neighbors.

  Summary: Fifteen tales of Johnny Chuck, Sammy Jay, Jimmy Skunk, and the other animals and birds of the Green Meadow. This is a reprinting of the book first published in 1913.
  1. Children's stories, American.   [1. Animals–Fiction]   I. Cady, Harrison, 1877–   ill.   II. Title.
PZ7.B917Mo 1984   [Fic]   68-21862
ISBN 0-316-11656-4

Published simultaneously in Canada
By Little, Brown & Company (Canada) Limited

Contents

Foreword

No writer has opened the eyes of so many children to the world of nature as the late Thornton W. Burgess. In the process of telling stories about the many creatures of the wild, he also helped children to understand themselves better and to grow.

Although writing for children was to become his lifework, he began writing in the magazine world of adults. His first children's stories were written merely to entertain his own son, who was off visiting grandparents. In 1910, these stories and a few others were published under the title *Old Mother West Wind*. It was a turning point in Mr. Burgess's life.

Two years afterward the first of his children's bedtime stories appeared in the newspapers. These short nature stories were to continue uninterrupted six days a week for forty-four years. There were to be many books as well, some collections of the newspaper stories, others completely new. Burgess was a prodigious writer.

Today's children love his stories as much as the youngsters of the 1920's did. The magic of a fine storyteller lives on, and no children's nature writer has come along to take his place. Maybe this is because he discovered a key to reaching children and seriously applied himself to the task of helping them grow into sound adults. In his autobiography, *Now I Remember,* Burgess describes what he was attempting to do with his children's stories.

"To be honest with myself," he wrote, "it would be a bit altruistic to say that in the beginning the primary purpose behind the stories I wrote was specifically anything more than making a living in a congenial line of work. They were simple little animal stories written for the sole purpose of entertaining small readers. However, from the start they were based on truth, the facts in regard to habits and characteristics of the characters involved. They were designed to entertain, education being wholly incidental.

"As the success of the stories grew my own education began. Gradually I awoke to the understanding that entertainment was in truth incidental, merely the means to an important end; that I was in possession of the master key to education along many and diverse lines; that Nature is the universal teacher."

I am among the millions for whom Burgess's key unlocked new worlds. Along with the others I learned the basic facts about the lives of our wild neighbors from these stories. I also learned much, quite unwittingly, about such human traits as curiosity, kindness, thrift, courage and wisdom. Animal nature was the warp of his tales, human nature the woof.

Although most people associate Burgess with stories for children of the primary grades, he wrote for older children as well. When I had outgrown the *Old Mother West Wind* stories, but hardly my interest in natural history, I searched for books that would teach me more about birds and mammals. I found little at my age level until the librarian guided me back to the Burgess shelf and showed me *The Burgess Book of Birds* and *The Burgess Book of Animals*. Inside the covers of these books the familiar characters of the bedtime stories took on a new dimension and the superb paintings of the great wildlife artist Louis Agassiz Fuertes became my guide for field identification for years to come. There are many more good natural-history books for nine-to-eleven-year-olds today, but in my opinion these two books have not yet been surpassed.

Burgess was a fine naturalist as well as a writer and he kept alert to new knowledge throughout his long life. He wrote his last book when he was ninety years old and it was as up-to-date as any undertaken by someone just out of college. Written for somewhat older children, this book, *The Burgess Book of Nature Lore,* presents the fundamentals of ecology.

In the bedtime stories Reddy Fox never catches Peter Rabbit. Of course a good storyteller doesn't want to lose a good character, and besides, who wants to put a young child to bed with a tale ending in blood and gore. Older children can more easily comprehend food chains emotionally, so we find them described in books for them. Burgess was a master of tailoring story to audience.

It is this very skill that has brought criticism upon his head from some people who have not taken the time to examine what he was doing. He is accused of the prime crime of nature writing — being anthropomorphic.

It is true that Burgess has his animals talk and that some of his illustrators put clothes on the animals they drew. In the period during which these drawings were made this was thought to give the animals charm. It was a fashion of the time, though it bothers many people today.

The stories themselves are not anthropomorphic in any sense that is likely to be damaging to the development of a child's attitudes toward other creatures and their environment. In the early nineteen hundreds, many scientists believed that animal behavior was very mechanistic and at the complete command of inherited physiological traits. But in recent years, the more careful and thorough studies of animal behaviorists such as Niko Tinbergen and Konrad Lorenz show a wide range of causes of animal behavior patterns and point out to us the animal origins and evolution of much human behavior that we once thought to be uniquely ours.

"The lives of our four-footed and feathered neighbors run parallel to our own," said Burgess. "What we experience, they experience, only in lesser degree. Keeping this in mind together with the fact that the child intuitively understands and recognizes his superiority, it becomes a simple matter to convey to the child any desired lesson through the medium of a story concerning a member of lesser orders. But there must be a rigid adherence to truth and fact in regard to these characters. It is because the child recognizes that the stories are true in all essentials that the lesson is at once taken home. Thus the story that humanizes the animal to the point of the impossible is bound to fail in its purpose from an educational standpoint. It is permissible for Peter Rabbit to talk because the child understands that in all probability there is some form of a communication between animals. But it is not permissible for Peter Rabbit to climb a tree or ride a bicycle. The child instantly senses the lack of truth and this of necessity weakens any lesson which the story may seek to convey."

Thornton Burgess made a great contribution to the education of youth. He taught them about the natural world around them and he helped instil in them attitudes and values which would enrich their lives. I for one lead a richer life because of the work of this humble gentleman.

With a nation growing increasingly more urban and thus divorced from direct experiences with the natural world that sustain us physically and often spiritually, it is important that the youngsters of today have stories such as these to bring them closer to an understanding of the world of nature.

Charles E. Roth
Director of Education
Massachusetts Audubon Society

When MOTHER WEST WIND'S NEIGHBORS
Was First Published in 1913,
the Dedication Read as Follows:

To the Silent Partner
Whose Faith, Helpful Criticisms
and Never Failing Optimism Are a
Perpetual Source of Inspiration
MY WIFE

Why Johnny Chuck Does Not Like Blacky the Crow

1

Johnny Chuck sat in his doorway and watched the world go by. It was a very pleasant world, a very pleasant world indeed, thought Johnny Chuck. Everyone was out that pleasant May morning. Johnny Chuck had slipped from his bed early, but before he had washed himself Jimmy Skunk had stuck his head in at the door and shouted: "Good morning, Johnny Chuck!"

Johnny Chuck had said "Good morning, Jimmy Skunk," had finished dressing, and then gone out to get his breakfast. Far, far away beyond the Green Meadows, Old Mother West Wind was just beginning to turn a great windmill to pump water for some thirsty cows in Farmer Brown's barnyard. The

Merry Little Breezes were hopping and skipping over to the Smiling Pool to pay their respects to Great-Grandfather Frog. Old Mr. Toad already was at work in his garden. Yes, it surely was a very pleasant world.

Johnny Chuck ate his breakfast and then sat on his doorstep. His heart was light, for he possessed the best thing in the world, which is contentment. Pretty soon he saw Blacky the Crow fly over to Farmer Brown's cornfield and begin to pull up the tender young corn.

"Dear me, dear me, Blacky the Crow is sure to get into trouble," thought Johnny Chuck.

Sure enough, Blacky the Crow did get into trouble. Johnny Chuck saw a puff of smoke over in the cornfield. Then he heard a loud bang, and Blacky the Crow rose into the air in a hurry. As he flew, three black feathers floated down to the ground. Blacky the Crow had been shot by Farmer Brown's boy, who had been hiding in the cornfield. But Blacky was more frightened than hurt, and he flew across the Green Meadows to the Lone Pine to nurse his hurts and his temper.

Now it is seldom that anyone can get into trouble without getting someone else into trouble also. If Blacky the Crow had let Farmer Brown's corn alone, Farmer Brown's boy would not have come out with his gun. But now that he was

out with his gun, he thought he would find something else to shoot at, just for fun.

He remembered Johnny Chuck's house, so he began to creep up very, very carefully to try to catch Johnny Chuck napping. Now Johnny Chuck had done no harm, so he did not suspect harm from Farmer Brown's boy. Instead of watching him, Johnny Chuck settled himself comfortably to watch the antics of the Field Mice children at play.

Suddenly up rushed one of the Merry Little Breezes quite out of breath.

"Get into your house, Johnny Chuck, quick!" he cried.

Long, long ago Johnny Chuck had learned to obey first and ask questions later. Now he didn't so much as turn his head to see what the trouble might be, but turned a back somersault down his doorway. Just then there was a terrible "bang," and the sand at the entrance to Johnny Chuck's house was blown in all directions by the shot. But Johnny Chuck was safe down below. Farmer Brown's boy had been just too late.

Poor Johnny Chuck! His heart went pit-a-pat, pit-a-pat, pit-a-pat, and he trembled all over. He was dreadfully frightened. All the joy of the beautiful sunshiny day was gone. He didn't dare stick so much as the tip of his little black nose out of his door for fear that Farmer Brown's boy was waiting there with his gun. Worse still, he knew that Farmer Brown's boy knew of his snug little home and so, of course, it was no longer safe. He had to go out and make a new home. Yes, Sir,

6

Johnny Chuck had got to move, and all because Blacky the Crow had been in mischief.

Now just as Johnny Chuck suspected, Farmer Brown's boy sat down to wait for Johnny to come out. He loaded his gun, and then he sat very still, watching Johnny Chuck's doorway. The Merry Little Breezes saw him sitting there, and they were afraid, terribly afraid, that Johnny Chuck would come out. And if he did — what, oh, what could they do?

Then one of them had an idea, such a bright idea! In a flash he had rushed over and snatched the big straw hat from the head of Farmer Brown's boy. All the other Merry Little Breezes clapped their hands for joy. They remembered how they once had saved Mrs. Redwing's speckled eggs, so they all joined in and took turns kicking the old straw hat ahead of them across the Green Meadows. It made a splendid football, that old straw hat, and in the fun of kicking it they almost forgot what had started the new game.

Of course Farmer Brown's boy put his gun down and ran after his hat. The Merry Little Breezes would sometimes let him just touch it with the tips of his fingers, but he never could quite get hold of it. Finally the Merry Little Breezes, lifting all together, took the old hat up, up, up, and sailing it out over the Smiling Pool, dropped it right over the big green

7

lily pad on which Great-Grandfather Frog was dozing and dreaming of the days when the world was young.

"Chugarum," shouted Grandfather Frog, and dived with a great splash into the Smiling Pool, to come up on the other side that he might see what it was that had fallen from a clear sky over his big green lily pad.

While Farmer Brown's boy cut a long pole and with it fished in the Smiling Pool for his old straw hat, one of the Merry Little Breezes hurried back to Johnny Chuck's house to tell him that the way was clear, and that it was quite safe for him to come out. You may be sure Johnny Chuck was glad, very glad to hear that. Very, very cautiously he poked his little black nose out of his doorway. Way down by the Smiling Pool he could see Farmer Brown's boy fishing for his old straw hat. Johnny Chuck didn't wait to see him get it. No, Sir! Johnny Chuck just whispered "Good-by" to his snug little home and scampered up the Lone Little Path as fast as he could.

Pretty soon he came to a secret little path he had made for just such a need; no one knew of it but himself. The secret little path led to a spot Johnny Chuck had long before picked out for a new home, if ever he should need one.

Without wasting a minute, he began to dig as never had he dug before. My, how the sand did fly!

Late that afternoon Johnny Chuck's new home was finished and Johnny Chuck sat in his doorway looking over the Green Meadows and watching the world go by. It was a very beautiful world, a very beautiful world indeed, thought Johnny Chuck. His new home was even better than his old one, and he was sure that no one knew of the secret little path that led to it. He was happy, was Johnny Chuck, for once more he had found the best thing in the world, which is contentment.

Presently he saw Farmer Brown's boy coming down the Lone Little Path across the Green Meadows. With him was another boy, and they each carried two pails of water. Johnny Chuck sat up very straight to watch.

Down the Lone Little Path went Farmer Brown's boy and the other boy, straight to Johnny Chuck's old home. First they put a big stone over what used to be Johnny Chuck's back door. Then they began to pour water down the front door. They were trying to drown out Johnny Chuck. Back and forth, back and forth they went, lugging the heavy pails of water.

Johnny Chuck chuckled as he watched them. But, oh, how thankful he was that he had moved so promptly that morning, and how grateful to the Merry Little Breezes he felt for their help.

After a time the boys gave it up and trudged wearily up the Lone Little Path with their empty pails. Johnny Chuck laughed softly to himself as he watched them go. Then he trotted down his secret little path to the Lone Little Path and down the Lone Little Path onto the Green Meadows, where the Merry Little Breezes were at play, to thank them for what they had done for him that day and to join them in a last mad frolic before Old Mother West Wind should take them to their home behind the Purple Hills.

"Caw, caw, caw," said Blacky the Crow, flying over to the Lone Pine.

"Now I wonder who he is making trouble for," thought Johnny Chuck.

And this is why Johnny Chuck does not love Blacky the Crow.

Unc' Billy Possum Arrives

2

There was another stranger in the Green Forest. Where he came from or who he was no one knew. The Merry Little Breezes had found him very busily examining a hollow tree, just as if he meant to stay. They watched him for a few minutes, then hurried off to spread the news. Peter Rabbit was the first they met, and Peter listened gravely as, all talking at once, they told him about the stranger.

When the Merry Little Breezes had hurried on, Peter started for the Green Forest. Peter went on tiptoe as he approached the hollow tree. He wanted to see the stranger before the stranger saw him. No one was in sight. Peter sat down behind a stump and waited. Pretty soon a funny face was

H.CADY

poked out of the hollow tree. Peter had to clap his hands over his mouth to keep from laughing right out. It was the face of a little old man, a sharp little face with a sharp little nose, that looked as if it might poke into anybody's business.

The stranger looked this way and that way. Then he came out of the hollow, where Peter could have a good look at him. He wore a suit of grayish white, a rough, tumbled suit of which he seemed to take no care at all. He wore black gloves and black stockings through which his white fingers and toes showed. And he had a long tail, a tail that looked very like the long tails of the Rat family, only it was much larger. Altogether the stranger looked quite innocent and harmless and Peter decided to make himself known.

"Good morning," said Peter, stepping out from behind the stump.

The stranger looked down at him and grinned. "Mornin', Suh," said he.

"May I ask where you come from and how long you are going to stay?" asked Peter Rabbit in his most polite manner, and Peter can be very polite when he wants to be.

The stranger showed all his teeth again in another grin. "Yo' may," said he. "Ah reckons yo' alls doan know me. Ah comes from ol' Virginny, and this place is so like mah ol' home that Ah reckon Ah'll stay. Some folks calls me Ol' Bill Possum, but most folks calls me Unc' Billy."

"I'm pleased to know you, Uncle Billy, and I hope you'll like the Green Forest and the Green Meadows," said Peter.

Unc' Billy chuckled. "Ah's right sho' Ah shall," he replied. Then he leaned over and very slowly winked at Peter Rabbit. "Can yo' tell me, Suh, if any poultry live around here?" he asked.

Peter looked a wee bit puzzled. "If you are asking about hens," he replied, "Farmer Brown has some very fine ones over beyond the Green Meadows."

Unc' Billy winked again. "Ah'm right sho' Ah'll stay," said he.

Peter Rabbit and the Merry Little Breezes soon had the news spread not only all through the Green Forest itself but all over the Green Meadows. Of course everybody soon found some excuse to visit the hollow tree where Unc' Billy Possum had decided to make his home.

Unc' Billy was tired after his long journey and was fast asleep inside the hollow tree when the first of the callers arrived, so they sat down around the foot of the tree to wait. Every few minutes another visitor would arrive. Each would appear very much surprised to find the others there and would

look a little foolish. Each pretended that it was merely chance that had brought him that way. But no one seemed to have business important enough to take him away, and pretty soon nearly all the little people of the Green Forest and Green Meadows were seated at the foot of the hollow tree.

Finally Johnny Chuck grew tired of waiting. "I begin to believe that we have been fooled and that there isn't any stranger here at all," said he.

"There is, too, for I talked with him," said Peter Rabbit indignantly.

"If you know him, why don't you call him out so we can all meet him?" asked Jimmy Skunk.

"I — I — I don't think it would be polite," replied Peter

Rabbit. But this wasn't the real reason. Down in his heart Peter was just a wee bit afraid. You see, he didn't know as the stranger would like it, and Peter had looked up at some very sharp teeth when Unc' Billy Possum had grinned down on him that morning.

"Let's send Chatterer the Red Squirrel up to look in and see if there is anyone in the hollow tree," said Reddy Fox.

"No, you don't, Reddy Fox!" shouted Chatterer, who is quick-tempered and a terrible scold, and he began to call Reddy names in such a shrill voice that he waked Unc' Billy.

Very slowly Unc' Billy Possum climbed out of the hollow where all could see him. He looked down, and then he grinned until he showed all his white teeth.

"How do yo' alls do?" asked Unc' Billy. " 'Pears to me that yo' alls are right smart interested in mah ol' hollow tree."

"It isn't the hollow tree; it's yourself, Uncle Billy," explained Peter Rabbit. "These are your new neighbors come to make a call."

Unc' Billy grinned again. "Ah cert'nly feel honored. Ah think Ah will come down and shake hands," said he.

Danny Meadow Mouse looked at Unc' Billy's white teeth and remembered that he couldn't stop any longer. So did Striped Chipmunk and Whitefoot the Wood Mouse. In fact,

by the time Unc' Billy reached the ground there was no one there but Reddy Fox. But as they left, each had promised to call again.

Unc' Billy grinned at Reddy Fox and showed all his teeth once more.

"I'm pleased to meet you, Mr. Possum," said Reddy respectfully, which wasn't at all what he had meant to say, and then he started off to tell Granny Fox all about it.

It was a few days later that Jimmy Skunk felt a great emptiness in his stomach. Jimmy sat down and gently rubbed his stomach, as he tried to decide what would taste best for his supper.

"Let me see," said Jimmy, "I had beetles for breakfast and grasshoppers for dinner, and now for supper I want a change. What shall it be?"

Just then a sleepy "cockadoodledoo" sounded from way over towards Farmer Brown's. Jimmy Skunk rubbed his stomach and chuckled softly. "It's an egg I want; it certainly is an egg, maybe two, perhaps three."

The black shadows crept out from the Purple Hills across the Green Meadows. Jimmy watched them impatiently. How slow they were! He did wish they would hurry. With every little minute he grew hungrier. It wouldn't do to go up to

Farmer Brown's hen house until it was so dark that Farmer Brown's boy would have gone into the house.

Slowly the shadows crept up towards the hen house, until finally it was all in darkness. Softly Jimmy Skunk crept up to a hole of which he knew. Just outside he sat down and listened for a few minutes. He could hear the biddies clucking sleepily. When all was still, Jimmy Skunk crept inside, and if you had been there to see, you would have found him wearing his broadest smile, for, I am sorry to say, Jimmy Skunk felt quite at home in Farmer Brown's hen house.

"Let me see, old Mrs. Speckles lays the largest eggs, and young Mrs. Topknot lays the sweetest eggs, and old Mrs. Featherlegs lays the most beautiful eggs. I think I'll try Mrs. Topknot's first," said Jimmy to himself.

He went straight to Mrs. Topknot's nest and reached in. It was empty. Jimmy made a wry face and hurried over to the nest of Mrs. Speckles. Not an egg could be felt. Jimmy's heart sank. Could it be that Farmer Brown's boy had gathered the eggs before dark? It must be, though he usually gathered them in the morning. Jimmy hurried over to the nest of Mrs. Featherlegs. Ha! What was that? It was an egg! Jimmy reached in with both hands to take it out. How queer and light it felt! Jimmy's fingers slipped around to one end.

There was a hole there! Jimmy was holding nothing but an empty shell.

Then Jimmy Skunk knew that it was not Farmer Brown's boy who had been before him, but someone who likes eggs as well as he does. For a minute Jimmy lost his temper and ground his teeth, he was so angry.

"It must be that glutton, Shadow the Weasel," he muttered, as he began to search in all the other nests within reach. Not an egg was to be found.

Now there were a lot of nests that Jimmy couldn't reach, for he is not a climber. He was looking up at these hungrily when he noticed something hanging from one of them. He reached up and gave it a sharp pull. Down, right on top of Jimmy Skunk, tumbled Unc' Billy Possum with a big egg in his hands!

Jimmy was so startled that he started to run. Then he turned to look back. There lay Unc' Billy flat on his back, grinning and trying to get his breath.

"Good evening, Suh. These are monstrous fine eggs yo' alls have so convenient, Suh," said Unc' Billy Possum.

When Jimmy Skunk found that it was Unc' Billy Possum who had been before him in Farmer Brown's hen house and stolen all the eggs within reach from the ground, he was mad.

"What are you doing here?" he demanded.

"Enjoying mahself most amazingly, Suh," replied Unc' Billy, patting the freshly laid egg he was holding.

"You've got no business here!" said Jimmy fiercely, for the sight of that egg Unc' Billy was holding so tightly made his stomach feel emptier than ever, and that was very empty indeed.

"Ah beg yo' pardon, but may Ah ask what business brings yo' here?" asked Unc' Billy, and his grin grew broader than ever.

"I — I — I — " Jimmy didn't know just what to say.

Unc' Billy chuckled. "Ah guess your business and mah business in this hen house would amount to the same thing if we were to ask Farmer Brown, and he would say that we hadn't any business here at all," said he. Then he rolled the egg he was holding over to Jimmy Skunk. "Ah done eat all Ah can hold, so Ah takes pleasure in giving this to yo'," and once more Unc' Billy grinned.

At first Jimmy Skunk thought that he would refuse the egg. But Jimmy is very fair-minded. He knew perfectly well that Unc' Billy Possum had just as much right to those eggs as he had, and that neither of them had any right to them at all. But then, Jimmy couldn't see that Farmer Brown or his boy had any right to them, either. They really belonged to Mrs. Topknot and Mrs. Speckles and Mrs. Featherlegs. So when Unc' Billy rolled the egg over to him, Jimmy allowed his temper to cool off. There wasn't another egg within reach, for Jimmy had searched in every nest he could look into. This egg certainly did look good. Jimmy suddenly held out his hand to Unc' Billy.

"You are right, Uncle Billy," said he. "I guess you have just as much business here as I have. You certainly have the advantage of me, because you can climb while I cannot. I'm much obliged to you for this egg, because without it I should go hungry."

In a flash Unc' Billy Possum was on his feet, and two seconds later he was scrambling up to the top row of nests. He was down again with another egg by the time Jimmy had finished the first one. He gave it to Jimmy with a low and very polite bow.

"Ah have the honor to propose that we become partners, Suh, and that in honor of the new firm of Skunk & Possum we each eat another egg," said Unc' Billy, his eyes twinkling.

And they did.

Why Ol' Mistah Buzzard Has a Bald Head

3

Ol' Mistah Buzzard had come up from the South to live in the Green Forest, so as to be near his old friend, Unc' Billy Possum. At first all the little folks of the Green Forest and all the little people of the Green Meadows had been a little bit suspicious of the big black bird sailing round and round high up in the blue, blue sky, and the littlest ones had had a great fear, for he looked so much like Redtail the Hawk that they thought he must be at the very least Redtail's own cousin. When Unc' Billy Possum heard this, he hurried around telling everyone that Ol' Mistah Buzzard was a friend of his and that he wouldn't harm anyone for the world.

Then among the little forest and meadow people there was great rejoicing, and they all hurried over to the tall dead tree in the Green Forest, where Ol' Mistah Buzzard delighted to sit, to tell him how glad they were that he had come to make his home in the Green Forest. Unc' Billy Possum was on hand to introduce them, and each one was very polite to Ol' Mistah Buzzard, especially the littlest ones who had been most frightened when they had first seen him sailing high up in the blue, blue sky.

Ol' Mistah Buzzard was just as polite as they were, and bowed his wrinkled bald head to this one and bowed his wrinkled bald head to that one in a very grand manner. As usual, Peter Rabbit was brimming over with curiosity. He could hardly wait to be introduced before he began to ask questions.

"I beg your pardon, Mistah Buzzard, but will you tell us if you are very, very old?" Peter asked, just as soon as he had a chance.

Ol' Mistah Buzzard gave Peter a funny, sidewise look and slyly winked at Unc' Billy Possum as he replied:

"Ah reckon Ah'm right smart old, Brer Rabbit. Yes, Suh, Ah reckon Ah'm right smart old. But Ah might be older; Ah sho'ly might be older. Why do yo' ask, Brer Rabbit?"

Peter looked a little bit foolish, just a little bit foolish, and he hesitated before he replied in a very low voice:

"Because I thought that only very old people ever have bald heads."

Ol' Mistah Buzzard threw back his head and laughed and laughed and laughed, fit to kill himself. "Ha, ha, ha! Ho, ho, ho!" laughed Ol' Mistah Buzzard.

And because he seemed so tickled, everybody else began to laugh, too. Even Peter Rabbit laughed, although he felt very uncomfortable, because it seemed as if they were laughing at him.

"Ah reckon, Brer Rabbit, yo' all doan know much about mah family. Ah reckon yo' all done live so long up here in the No'th that yo' done got to thinking that no one who lives anywhere else is of much account. Isn't that so, Brer Rabbit?" said Ol' Mistah Buzzard, with another sly wink at Unc' Billy Possum.

Peter Rabbit looked more confused than ever, but he hastened to tell Ol' Mistah Buzzard that such a thought had never entered his head, and that he held the greatest respect, the very greatest respect, for Ol' Mistah Buzzard and all his family. Then, his curiosity getting the better of him, as it always does, he added:

26

"But I would like to know how it is that you happen to be bald-headed, Mistah Buzzard, when none of the other people whom I know are."

Ol' Mistah Buzzard grinned good-naturedly and settled himself more comfortably on a branch of the tall dead tree.

"It's quite a story, Brer Rabbit; it's quite a story!" said he.

"Do, please do tell it to us!" cried Peter Rabbit and Johnny Chuck and Happy Jack Squirrel together.

Ol' Mistah Buzzard looked all around the circle of little forest folks and meadow people.

"Ah doan want to tire yo' alls. Ah cert'nly doan want to tire yo' alls and make a nuisance of mahself, jes' when we alls are getting so nicely acquainted," said he.

"You won't! You won't! Please do tell us how it is you happen to be bald-headed!" shouted all together

Ol' Mistah Buzzard scratched his bald head gently, very gently. Then, while all the little forest folks and meadow people crowded closer about the foot of the tall dead tree, he cleared his throat and began:

"Once upon a time, long, long ago when the world was young, mah grandaddy a thousand times removed wore feathers on his haid. Yes, Suh, he wore feathers on his haid jes' the same as ol' King Eagle and Brer Redtail and Brer Falcon and all the other birds. He was ve'y proud of the feathers on his haid, was Grandaddy Buzzard, but he was still mo' proud of his big, broad wings. He cert'nly was proud of those big wings. He used to spend most of his time sailing round and round and round, way up in the sky, and jes' minding his own bus'ness.

"Ol' King Eagle was ve'y fierce and ve'y strong, jes' like Brer Eagle, whom yo' all know, is today. He was jealous, was ol' King Eagle, as he watched Grandaddy Buzzard sailing round and round and round up in the sky, 'cause he been taking notice that all the other birds done be watching Grandaddy Buzzard with adm'ration shining in their eyes. Yo' see ol' King Eagle didn't want anybody to be admired 'cepting hisself. One day he hear li'l' Mistah Sparrer say he wished he could fly like Grandaddy Buzzard. Ol' King Eagle he flare up right away.

" 'Pooh!' say ol' King Eagle. 'That no 'count Buzzard can't fly!'

"Li'l' Mistah Sparrer was sitting snug and safe in the middle of a thorn tree, and he was right pert and sassy, was li'l' Mistah Sparrer. Yes, Suh, he cert'nly was right pert and sassy, for he up and holler out:

" 'He can beat yo' flying any day, even if yo' are the king!'

28

"Yes, Suh, that's jes' what he done holler right out. A lot of the other birds heard him and ol' King Eagle he knew then that he jes' *have* to make sassy li'l' Mistah Sparrer swallow his own words. Pretty soon Grandaddy Buzzard come sailing down and light on the ol' daid tree where he always sit. Ol' King Eagle he come over and say they have a race to see who can fly the highest. Grandaddy Buzzard doan know nothing about what sassy li'l' Mistah Sparrer done say, but he willing to 'blige ol' King Eagle, and anyhow he doan want trouble nohow, so he say he willing to race ol' King Eagle.

"Ev'ybody come to see that race, ev'ybody what can fly or walk or creep. Ol' King Eagle he order his cousins, Brer Redtail the Hawk and Brer Falcon, to go 'long with him, but what fo' nobody know. By and by they start, ol' King Eagle, Brer Redtail, Brer Falcon, and Grandaddy Buzzard. They go round and round, up and up in the blue, blue sky, till ev'ybody grow dizzy jes' looking at 'em. Round and round, up and up in the blue, blue sky they climb and climb till they nothing more'n specks, and then pretty soon they go clear out of sight. Yes, Suh, they fly so high nobody see 'em fo' a long, long time.

"People getting tired of waiting when sharp-eyed, sassy li'l' Mistah Sparrer shout: 'Here they come!' Sure 'nuff li'l' Mis-

tah Sparrer is right. Way up in the blue, blue sky were some li'l' specks. They grew bigger and bigger and bigger. Then someone discovered that there were only three. Yes, Suh, there were only three. Pretty soon ol' King Eagle dropped down to earth and he was clean beat out, was ol' King Eagle, clean beat out. So was Brer Redtail and so was Brer Falcon. Yo' never did see three people mo' beat out than they were.

" 'Where's Mistah Buzzard?' shouted ev'ybody together.

"Ol King Eagle he bend his haid down and drop his wings and breathe mighty hard. Bimeby, when he get his breath, he say: 'Ah beat that no 'count Buzzard so bad he ashamed of hisself and fly away.' That's what ol' King Eagle say, and his cousins, Brer Redtail and Brer Falcon, they nod their haids and say it jes' so.

"Ev'ybody mighty disappointed in Grandaddy Buzzard, and they 'low ol' King Eagle was right and that Grandaddy Buzzard was no 'count, jes' like ol' King Eagle say. Jes' while they all talking about it and getting ready to go home, sassy li'l' Mistah Sparrer he holler: 'Here he come now!' Ev'ybody look up, and sho' 'nuff there come Grandaddy Buzzard, sailing down and down and down right into the midst of 'em. He doan seem the least bit tired, and smile jes' like he always do when he been taking a li'l' pleasuring. Ev'yone begin to hoot at him till sassy li'l' Mistah Sparrer, sitting safe in the middle of the thorn tree, holler:

" 'What's the matter with yo' haid, Mistah Buzzard?'

"Grandaddy Buzzard look kind of foolish and feel of his haid like it mighty tender. 'Ah done sco'ch it, Ah guess,' he say, jes' like he was 'pologizing.

"Ev'ybody crowded round Grandaddy Buzzard to look. Sho' 'nuff, he hadn't got a feather left on his haid. No, Suh, not so much as one li'l' feather! Yo' see, he done fly so high he get too close to the sun, and it sco'ch 'em all off.

"When ol' King Eagle see that, he forget all about how tired he is, and he jes' sneak off while ev'ybody trying to shake hands with Grandaddy Buzzard all at once. Brer Redtail and Brer Falcon they sneak off after ol' King Eagle, for ev'ybody know by that time they been telling a lie to save their cousin, ol' King Eagle.

"And ever since that day when Grandaddy Buzzard beat ol' King Eagle, mah family has had bald haids," concluded Ol' Mistah Buzzard proudly.

Hooty the Owl Gets Even

4

"Caw, caw, caw!" That was Blacky the Crow. His cousin, Sammy Jay, heard him and straightway started for the big hemlock on the top of which Blacky the Crow was sitting. On the way, he stopped to tell all his relatives to come along as quickly as they could, so as not to miss the fun.

"He's found Hooty the Owl asleep, and we're going to have some fun," replied Sammy Jay.

"That's a shame," said Johnny Chuck indignantly. "You ought to be ashamed of yourself, Sammy Jay."

Sammy just stuck his tongue out at Johnny Chuck, flirted some dust off his blue and white coattails, and hurried on.

By the time he reached the big hemlock, all the crows of the Green Forest were there, and such a racket as they were making! Of course, they had waked up Hooty the Owl, and he was very cross, as people who are waked out of a sound sleep are apt to be. He sat with his back against the tree, and he puffed his feathers out until he looked three times as big as he really is.

"*Hooty is a coward!*
  Hooty is a thief!
If Hooty comes to my house,
  He'll surely come to grief!"

shouted Blacky, slipping up behind and pulling Hooty's coattails. Hooty snapped his bill and hissed fiercely. But he couldn't see very well because the sun was bright, and so Blacky had no trouble in keeping out of his way.

"Wait till it's dark, Blacky the Crow! You wait till it's dark!" snapped Hooty the Owl.

Blacky stopped teasing for a minute and shivered just a bit under his black coat. He knew how fierce Hooty was when he could see, and, to tell the truth, he really had rather not meet him after dark. Just then Sammy Jay flew almost into Hooty's face and cried:

> *"Hooty is a blind man!*
> *Hooty cannot see!*
> *Who's afraid of Hooty*
> *In the hemlock tree?"*

Blacky forgot all his fears, and once more led the tormentors of Hooty.

Now, Hooty was not only sleepy and half blind in the bright light, but his stomach was so full of good things that he could hardly move. So he just snapped and hissed and scolded, keeping his back against the tree until the crows and the jays grew tired of their fun, and one by one went about their business. As the last one, with a final jeer, flew away, Hooty the Owl settled himself to sleep again.

"Wait, just you wait," he muttered darkly.

"Good night, Hooty," cried one of the Merry Little Breezes, as he went hurrying through the Green Forest, just as jolly, round, red Mr. Sun was going to bed behind the Purple Hills.

"Good night," grumbled Hooty the Owl and blinked his big, round eyes. Then he blinked them again and shook out his feathers and yawned. He had had a good rest since the crows and the jays left him.

"Don't see what everybody goes to bed just at the best part of the day for," said Hooty to himself, for you know Hooty the Owl sleeps when the sun shines, and flies abroad when the shadows creep out from the Purple Hills.

Way over on the other side of the Green Forest, Blacky the Crow croaked sleepily, as he tucked his head under his wing. Blacky was very tired, for he had had a very, very busy day. He had pulled up a whole row of Farmer Brown's young corn. Then he had had that whole hour of fun tormenting Hooty the Owl, when the latter was so sleepy and blinded by sunlight that he could do nothing but hiss and snap his bill. Blacky chuckled as he thought of it. Then he closed his eyes and in two minutes was fast asleep.

Now, someone else heard that chuckle, and chuckled in reply, but very softly. It was Hooty the Owl. His big yellow eyes grew bigger and brighter, as he flew over the big pine where Blacky was sleeping. No one but Hooty could have seen the black rascal in his snug retreat. But Hooty saw, for his eyes are made for seeing in the dark.

Back and forth, as lightly as a feather, and as silently, Hooty sailed over the big pine until he was sure that Blacky was sound asleep. Then something happened. Oh my, yes, something certainly did happen! Blacky the Crow was knocked off his perch and fell halfway to the ground before he could catch himself.

"C-a-a-w, c-a-a-a-w, c-a-a-w!" screamed Blacky in great fright. "Oh, dear, oh, dear! What was that?" he cried.

Blacky fluttered back up to his perch, bumping his head as he went, for it was so dark he couldn't see. Hardly had he comfortably settled himself once more and begun to doze, when off he went just as before. He was so frightened that he didn't know what to do, but, just as before, he fluttered back up to his perch. Not the tiniest sound was to be heard. Blacky turned his head this way and turned his head that way, and watched and listened and shivered and shook, but not a thing could he hear. Yet, just as soon as he closed his eyes, some-

thing pushed him off his perch and tumbled him down. At first he had thought that he had had a bad dream, but now he realized that something was coming out of the darkness and tormenting him. After a while he heard a voice from the top of the next tree. It was a very deep voice.

"How do you like it, Blacky?" asked the voice.

At first Blacky didn't recognize it. Then all of a sudden it came to him that this was Hooty the Owl, and that Hooty the Owl was getting even for the teasing which Blacky had given him that morning.

When Hooty had grown tired of teasing Blacky the Crow, he flew back and forth, back and forth, through the Green Forest, until he found Sammy Jay. Then Hooty teased Sammy Jay, just as he had Blacky the Crow, until he had frightened him almost to death. And just as the first faint light of morning came stealing across the Green Meadows, Hooty the Owl flew to the thickest part of the Green Forest to settle down for the day.

"My, but I have had a good time," said Hooty the Owl, with a chuckle, "and now I guess I'm even with Blacky the Crow and Sammy Jay."

Happy Jack Squirrel's Stolen Nuts

5

Something was wrong with Happy Jack Squirrel. There was no doubt about it; something was very wrong indeed with Happy Jack! He was racing up and down the old hollow chestnut tree, now in it, now out, now running round and round it, and all the time scolding as fast as his tongue could go. His voice grew angrier and angrier, and then all at once he sat down in his doorway, buried his face in his hands, and began to cry.

"Boo, hoo, hoo!" sobbed Happy Jack Squirrel.

Just then along came Chatterer the Red Squirrel, who is a cousin to Happy Jack the Gray Squirrel. Chatterer is a mischief-maker. He likes to see other people in trouble. As

soon as he saw Happy Jack sitting in his doorway crying, he put his hands on his hips, ran out his tongue at Happy Jack, and called shrilly:

> *"Crybaby Cripsey!*
> *His mammy's name is Dipsey!"*

Happy Jack stopped crying. "I'm not a crybaby!" he shouted.

"I bet you'd cry if someone had stolen all the nuts you had been hiding away for winter!"

Chatterer grinned. He does not love his cousin, Happy Jack, and it tickled him immensely to think that someone had stolen Happy Jack's nuts. Happy Jack saw that grin. He glared at Chatterer, then he said slowly: "I believe that you know where my nuts are."

"Perhaps I do and perhaps I don't," replied Chatterer provokingly.

"You're a thief!" cried Happy Jack.

"I'm not!"

"You are!"

"I'm not!"

"You are!"

There they were facing each other, two little cousins, one in a gray suit and the other in red, both so angry that they danced up and down. It wasn't pretty to see nor nice to hear.

Suddenly Happy Jack sprang at Chatterer. "I'll teach you to steal my nuts!" he cried.

Now Happy Jack is twice as big as his cousin, Chatterer, and the latter had no idea of fighting. So away he raced out on the very tip of a branch of the old chestnut and made a flying leap over into the next tree, and after him ran Happy

Jack, crying: "Stop thief! Stop thief!" at the top of his lungs.

My, but that was an exciting race through the treetops! But Happy Jack couldn't catch his nimble cousin, who, just to tease him, kept always just out of reach. Finally they stopped to rest in the old apple tree under which sat Peter Rabbit and Johnny Chuck.

"What's all this fuss about?" asked Peter Rabbit.

"He stole my nuts," said Happy Jack, pointing at Chatterer.

"No such thing," sputtered Chatterer.

Peter Rabbit turned to Johnny Chuck and winked one eye. Then he held up a warning hand. "Listen," said he. Way off in the Green Forest they heard a voice crying: "Thief, thief, thief!" It was Sammy Jay's voice.

Happy Jack understood then who had stolen his nuts. He held out his hand to Chatterer. "I take it all back," he said.

Chatterer grinned. "What will you give me if I'll find your nuts for you?" he asked.

"Half," replied Happy Jack.

"Agreed," said Chatterer, as he scampered off towards home.

He brushed his coat and combed his hair and put on his finest white waistcoat. Then he started along the Lone Little Path that twists and winds through the Green Forest. Presently he met Bobby Coon.

"Good morning, Bobby Coon," said Chatterer, with his very best bow. Bobby Coon looked at Chatterer sharply. When Chatterer is polite, you may be pretty sure that he has some favor to ask.

"Morning," growled Bobby Coon.

44

Chatterer pretended not to notice Bobby Coon's grumpy manner. "They tell me that you are a great traveler and have seen much of the world, Bobby Coon," said he. "It must be fine to have seen so much."

Now Bobby Coon felt greatly flattered to hear Chatterer say this. He swelled himself out in a very important manner and cleared his throat. "Yes," he boasted, "there isn't much in the Green Forest or on the Green Meadows that I don't know about. I know where everybody lives and — "

"Oh, Bobby Coon, it can't be that you know where everybody lives! That really can't be, for some folks are so very clever in hiding their homes," said Chatterer, pretending to be very doubtful.

"Pooh!" said Bobby Coon disdainfully. "There is no one so clever that he can hide his house from me!"

"Not even Sammy Jay?" asked Chatterer, with an air of great doubt.

"Ho, ho, ho!" laughed Bobby Coon. "Why, Sammy Jay lives in the little spruce tree that stands halfway down the hill between the Crooked Little Path and the Great Pine."

This was all that Chatterer wanted to know, so he bade Bobby Coon good-by and started on his way. As soon as Bobby Coon was out of sight, Chatterer hurried over to the young spruce halfway down the hill, and sure enough, there was Sammy Jay's home. Chatterer grinned, an unpleasant grin. "I think I'll make a call," said he.

In a flash he was up the tree. He had forgotten all his politeness now, for without so much as knocking he popped his head over the edge of Sammy Jay's nest and frightened Mrs. Jay so that she flew off screaming at the top of her lungs. But in a few minutes she was back, for she had left four beautiful eggs, and she knew that Chatterer is very fond of eggs.

"They are very nice eggs," said Chatterer.

"Yes," said Mrs. Jay, fearful of what he might say next.

"I'm very hungry," said Chatterer.

Mrs. Jay fell to weeping.

"Of course I'd rather have nuts, but I think that these will make me a very good dinner. Nuts are very scarce at this time of year."

Mrs. Jay stopped weeping. "Will you leave my eggs alone if I'll bring you some nuts?" she asked.

Chatterer agreed, and Mrs. Jay hurried off. As soon as her back was turned, Chatterer stole after her. "Now," he said, "I shall find out where Happy Jack's stolen nuts are."

Mrs. Jay went directly to the big pine where Blacky the Crow's old nest was. Chatterer hid behind a big gray birch and watched. His eyes shone. He was so excited that he could hardly keep his claws from rattling on the bark. Up in Blacky the Crow's old nest Mrs. Jay was very busy, very busy indeed. Every few minutes she would look all around to see if anyone was watching. She did not see Chatterer, and he chuckled to himself. Pretty soon she flew towards home.

Chatterer chuckled right out loud. Then like a flash he climbed the big pine to the old nest of Blacky the Crow, and there he found — what do you think? Why, all Happy Jack Squirrel's store of nuts. Chatterer's eyes glistened. His cousin, Happy Jack, had promised him half if he would find and return them. Now he had found them and half were his. But why not more than half? Who would know if he did not divide fairly? Just as Mrs. Jay had done, Chatterer looked all around. No one was in sight.

Chatterer began to work very fast. Out of the bottom of the nest he pulled a lot of sticks, until pretty soon down dropped a nut and then another and another and another. By and by the last nut had dropped down to the ground. Chatterer scampered down and gathered them up into three piles instead of two. When the last nut had been picked up, he took all that were in one pile and hid them in a hollow log lying near. Then he hurried to find his cousin, Happy Jack, and show him the two piles of nuts.

"Oh, dear, how will we ever get all these nuts over to my hollow chestnut tree?" wailed Happy Jack. You see it was a long way over to the hollow chestnut tree, and Happy Jack could carry but two nuts at a time.

Chatterer winked one of his small, bright eyes. Then he whispered in one of Happy Jack's ears, and Happy Jack was so tickled that he shouted aloud. Off the two started to the Green Meadows. There they found the Merry Little Breezes and soon had them racing over the Green Meadows and through the Green Forest with invitations to a nut race that afternoon.

Of course no one would miss such a jolly affair as that, and early in the afternoon all the little meadow people and all the little forest folk had gathered by the two piles of nuts. That is, all were there but Sammy Jay. You see Sammy's conscience troubled him, for you remember that he was the thief who stole the nuts in the first place.

When all were ready, Chatterer gave the word to start, and then everyone took as many nuts as he could carry and hurried over to Happy Jack's storehouse. Back and forth they scurried. Even Spotty the Turtle entered the race, although

H CADY

he moves so slowly that it took him all the afternoon to carry one nut.

When Happy Jack's pile had disappeared, they took Chatterer's over to his storehouse. And all the time Chatterer pretended to be very busy himself, but really wasn't doing a thing. It was very exciting, very exciting indeed. And who do you think won? Why, Peter Rabbit, because his legs are long and meant for hurrying.

When the last one had gone, Chatterer brushed his clothes, and then, with a crafty smile, he stole over to the hollow log where he had hidden the third pile of nuts. He was thinking how smart he had been. It didn't trouble him a bit that he had been dishonest. He peeped into the hollow and then he rubbed his eyes. The nuts were not there!

Chatterer sat on the end of the hollow log and scratched his head. With his sharp little eyes he looked this way and looked that way. The more he looked, the less he saw. This certainly was the very log in the hollow of which he had hidden a third of the nuts that really belonged to his cousin, Happy Jack. Once more he crept into the hollow and searched and searched. Not a nut was to be found. It was very strange, very strange indeed.

Then Chatterer did a very foolish thing. He lost his temper.

Yes, Sir, Chatterer lost his temper. He rushed out of the hollow log and worked himself into such a rage that he made the leaves fly in every direction, and all the time he scolded as fast as his tongue could go.

"Hello, what's going on here?" said a voice.

Chatterer stopped long enough to glare at the speaker. It was Bobby Coon.

"Nothing's the matter!" snapped Chatterer.

Bobby Coon grinned. "Seems to me you make a terrible fuss over nothing," said he. "If I didn't know, I should think you had lost something." Bobby Coon grinned again in the most provoking way, and began to comb his whiskers.

Chatterer looked at him. Could it be that Bobby Coon knew what had become of those nuts? But Chatterer did not dare ask any questions, because you see he had stolen those nuts, and it wouldn't do to say a word about them. So he just snapped crossly: "There's nothing the matter, and it's none of your business, anyway!"

"All right," said Bobby Coon good-naturedly, as he stretched lazily. "I guess I'll be going along.

"Folks who lose their tempers so
And all for nothing get so mad

H.CADY

Are best left quite alone, you know.
It really is, I think, too bad."

Bobby Coon went on down the Lone Little Path chuckling to himself, while Chatterer, crosser than ever, started anew to look for the missing nuts. Hardly had he begun when he heard another voice.

"I love to see folks rush about
So full of business all day long.
So be their work be honest work,
They'll soon make right of every wrong."

It was Jimmy Skunk, and he was talking to himself as he ambled down the Lone Little Path, just as if he didn't see Chatterer at all. Chatterer scowled as he watched Jimmy Skunk out of sight. Could it be that Jimmy knew anything about those nuts? Chatterer was growing very uncomfortable. He would go home and wait until tomorrow before looking any more. Chatterer's conscience was troubling him, and a troublesome conscience is a very uncomfortable thing.

No sooner was he out of sight than Striped Chipmunk popped out of a hole close by the old hollow log, and began the wildest dance ever seen, while his fat little sides shook with glee. You see, he had seen Chatterer hide the nuts, and

53

he knew that they were stolen. So while Chatterer had been planning the nut race, Striped Chipmunk had removed all the nuts to his own snug little storehouse, and tomorrow he would take them all back to his big cousin, Happy Jack.

> *"The world is very full of eyes;*
>   *They're in each rock and tree.*
> *Whate'er you do, be very sure*
>   *Someone is bound to see."*

So sang Striped Chipmunk, as he danced around the old hollow log.

Why Sammy Jay Cries "Thief"

6

"Thief! Thief! Thief!"

Such a harsh voice! And such an unpleasant thing to be screaming on a beautiful, sunshiny morning!

Johnny Chuck and Peter Rabbit looked up among the blossoms of the old apple tree. It seemed as if a bit of the sky itself was right there, in the midst of the pink and white flowers. It was Sammy Jay. His blue coat with white trimmings never looked handsomer, and the smart cap he always wears on his head never looked smarter. Yes, indeed, Sammy Jay was very beautiful to look at! Johnny Chuck thought so.

"What a handsome fellow Sammy Jay is!" he exclaimed admiringly.

Sammy Jay heard him and began to strut proudly and show off his fine coat.

"Handsome is as handsome does," said Peter Rabbit. "You heard what he was screaming?"

"Yes," said Johnny Chuck, "I heard; but whom was he calling a thief?"

Peter Rabbit turned and stared at Johnny Chuck as if he thought Johnny didn't know much. Then he looked up at Sammy Jay. "Tell Johnny Chuck what your name is!" he called.

Now Sammy Jay doesn't like Peter Rabbit and he flew into a rage at once. He leaned down and screamed at Peter at the top of his lungs, but all he could say was: "Thief! Thief! Thief!"

Peter grinned as he turned to Johnny Chuck. "When he screams 'Thief!' he's just telling all the world what he is himself," said Peter. "He's the worst thief on the Green Meadows or in the Green Forest. If you've got anything you really want to keep, don't let Sammy Jay see it."

"But what does he tell everybody that he is a thief for?" Johnny Chuck asked.

"He has to; Old Mother Nature makes him. I guess he can't help stealing. It runs in the family. His father was a thief, and his grandfather was a thief, and his great-grand-fathers way back to the days when the world was young were thieves," replied Peter Rabbit.

Just then Sammy Jay flew away, screaming "Thief!" at the top of his lungs.

"I wonder what mischief he's up to now. If there is any trouble anywhere on the Green Meadows or in the Green Forest that Sammy Jay isn't at the bottom of or doesn't know about, it is because Sammy was asleep when it happened. Sammy Jay is mighty fine to look at, but fine clothes never yet made a gentleman," said Peter Rabbit.

"But how did Old Mother Nature happen to make him tell everybody what he really is?" inquired Johnny Chuck.

Peter Rabbit yawned. "It's a long story," said he. "Some-day you go down to the Smiling Pool and ask Grandfather Frog to tell you all about it. He knows, for he told me. Now I must get back to the dear old briar patch for my morning nap. Good-by, Johnny Chuck."

"Good-by, Peter Rabbit," replied Johnny Chuck.

After Peter had left him for the dear old briar patch, Johnny sat on his doorstep under the old apple tree a long time, thinking of what Peter Rabbit had told him about Sammy Jay. "What a dreadful thing for anyone who is so handsome to be a thief, and how very, very dreadful to have to tell everybody!" said Johnny Chuck. "I believe I'll go over to the Smiling Pool right now and ask Grandfather Frog about it."

So Johnny Chuck brushed his clothes until he looked spick and span, and then he trotted down the Lone Little Path across the Green Meadows to the Smiling Pool. There, just as he expected, he found Grandfather Frog sitting on his own special big, green lily pad. Now Johnny Chuck is rather a favorite with Grandfather Frog, so when Johnny politely asked for the story of how it happens that Sammy Jay goes about crying "Thief!" Grandfather Frog was very willing to tell him.

"Chugarum!" began Grandfather Frog, in a very deep voice. "Chugarum! It was this way: A long, long time ago, a very long time ago, when the world was young, things were very different from what they are now. Oh, my, yes! Very different indeed! Everybody loved everybody else. At least, everybody was supposed to love everybody else. Nobody was afraid of anybody else, and all the animals and all the birds lived like one great happy family." Grandfather Frog sighed, and in his great, goggly eyes Johnny Chuck could see a dreamy look, as if he could really see those happy, long-ago

days when the world was young. Johnny waited patiently, and by and by Grandfather Frog began again.

"Old Mother Nature had given old Mr. Jay, the grandfather a thousand times removed of Sammy Jay, one of the handsomest coats of all the birds. It was just as if she had taken a little bit of the sky when it is bluest and trimmed it with little bits from the clouds when they are whitest."

"Just like Sammy Jay's beautiful coat now!" interrupted Johnny Chuck.

"Just like Sammy Jay's beautiful coat now," said Grandfather Frog. "At first old Mr. Jay, who wasn't old then, you know, but young and smart, didn't think anything about his handsome coat. After a while he noticed that whenever he came around, all the other animals and birds would stop whatever they were doing to admire his handsome coat. Pretty soon he began to admire it himself. The more he looked at it, the more he admired it. The more he admired it himself, the more he wanted others to admire it. Whenever anyone came near, he would strut back and forth, so as to show off his handsome suit.

"Now from admiring his clothes Mr. Jay got to admiring himself. He began to think that because Old Mother Nature had given him handsomer clothes than his neighbors had, he was a little better than they were. Then he began to look down on everyone who wasn't finely dressed. Yes, Sir, that is just the way Mr. Jay began to feel and act. Chugarum! Just as if fine clothes could ever make anyone any better than anyone else!" Grandfather Frog spoke with the greatest scorn.

"So Mr. Jay began to hold his head very high," continued Grandfather Frog. "He held it so high that when he met some of his neighbors who wore plain clothes, he didn't see them at all. At first they didn't mind. They laughed at him. But by and by they noticed that whenever Mr. Jay met any of his neighbors who wore fine clothes, such as Mr. Redbird and Mr. Tanager and Mr. Oriole, he always saw them and made them a very grand bow. Then these plain neighbors of Mr. Jay grew angry when he passed them with his head held so high and strutting so proudly to show off his beautiful blue and white suit. After a little while they just wouldn't have anything to do with him but made fun of him whenever he passed.

"But Mr. Jay didn't seem to mind. No, Sir, he didn't seem to mind, not the least little bit. You see he thought himself so far above these plain neighbors of his that he didn't care what they thought. Now you know fine clothes need a great

deal of care. So Mr. Jay began to spend more and more time in taking care of his fine coat. Indeed, he spent so much time in taking care of it and in thinking about it and showing it off, that he had very little time for anything else. He didn't even have time to work for his daily living. Besides, work would be apt to soil his fine coat. Work was for those who wore plain clothes. If they got them soiled, it wouldn't matter. But Mr. Jay had got to eat, even if he couldn't work. What do you think he did? Why, he began to steal from his neighbors. Yes, Sir, Mr. Jay began to steal!

"He was very sly about it, was Mr. Jay, and no one suspected him. So he stole what he wanted to eat and spent the rest of his time taking care of and showing off his fine clothes. I forgot to tell you that with his beautiful blue and white coat, Mr. Jay had a beautiful voice, one of the most beautiful voices among all the birds. He was almost as proud of his beautiful voice as he was of his coat. Even those who turned their backs to him because of his airs used to stop to listen when Mr. Jay sang. And this made Mr. Jay still more vain. So he went right on stealing from his neighbors and pretended to try to make himself believe that he had a right to take from his neighbors in return for the privilege of looking at his fine coat and listening to his beautiful voice.

64

"Now the habit of stealing is like all other bad habits; it grows and grows and grows. After a while Mr. Jay stole just for the fun of stealing. He stole more than he could possibly eat, and used to hide it away in all sorts of places. Whenever he found the storehouse of one of his neighbors, he would watch until he was sure that no one was looking. Then he would pick out the very best things in it, for nothing but the best was good enough for such a fine gentleman as he thought himself to be, and what he couldn't eat he would take to his own storehouse.

"Of course all this stealing couldn't go on without being found out. Mr. Jay's neighbors began to suspect each other. No one dreamed of suspecting Mr. Jay. He was too fine a gentleman to do anything like that! So they suspected each other, and matters grew from bad to worse until there was a terrible fuss among the animals and birds. Mr. Jay used to listen with his head on one side and chuckle to himself. He grew bolder and bolder, but he always took the greatest care to cover up his tracks. Oh, he was sly, was Mr. Jay!

"Now such a terrible state of affairs couldn't go on without reaching the ears of Old Mother Nature. One fine morning she appeared quite unexpectedly and called together all the animals and birds to tell her what the trouble was. My, how they did crowd around her, all talking at once, each accusing his neighbors of stealing from him! Only Mr. Jay had no complaint to make. He strutted up and down to show Old Mother Nature what good care he had taken of *his* fine suit, but he didn't have a word of complaint of anyone breaking into his storehouse. Old Mother Nature noticed this, and it didn't take her two minutes to guess who the thief was, for you can't fool Old Mother Nature, and it's of no use to try. She listened to all the complaints, then she made all the animals and birds sit down around her in a great circle. She told them how grieved she was that such a terrible thing should have happened, and how glad she was that she had come, for she had found the thief.

"When she said this Mr. Jay gave a guilty start. But Old Mother Nature didn't once look at him, and then he chuckled to himself and wondered whom she would accuse, and he chuckled still more as he saw what black looks his neighbors were giving each other. Then Old Mother Nature went on to say that she should punish the thief so that he never would forget it and so that none of his neighbors ever would forget it.

" 'But before I do this,' said Old Mother Nature, 'I am going to ask Mr. Jay to sing for us.'

"Of course Mr. Jay was prouder than ever to have Old

66

Mother Nature pay him such attention. He flew up to the top of the tallest tree, where everybody could see and admire his beautiful coat. He turned around two or three times as if trying to get a comfortable perch, but really to show himself off, and then he opened his mouth to sing. What do you think happened? Instead of the beautiful song that everybody expected and was waiting for, there came from Mr. Jay's throat only a harsh, unpleasant scream, and what he said was 'Thief! Thief! Thief!'

"Of course everybody knew who the thief was. Mr. Jay hid himself in the deepest, darkest part of the forest and hoped that the others would forget. But they never did. They couldn't have if they had tried, because forever after, whenever Mr. Jay tried to speak, he screamed 'Thief!' Old Mother Nature allowed him to keep his beautiful suit and pass it down to his children and his children's children, but ever since that long-ago day when the world was young, the Jays have had to tell the world just what they are. And now you know why it is that Sammy Jay cries 'Thief! Thief! Thief!' It is because his fine coat covers a black heart," concluded Grandfather Frog.

The Most Beautiful Thing in the World

7

Old Mother West Wind came down from the Purple Hills while the dew still lay heavy on the grass. She turned her Merry Little Breezes out to play on the Green Meadows and then, because she was in no hurry that pleasant morning, she stopped at the Smiling Pool to speak with Grandfather Frog.

"Good morning, Old Mother West Wind. Isn't this a beautiful morning?" said Grandfather Frog.

"It is indeed," replied Old Mother West Wind, "and there are many other beautiful things, Grandfather Frog. Do you know, I've just seen the most beautiful thing in the whole world."

"Where?" asked Grandfather Frog.

"Over in the old briar patch," replied Old Mother West Wind.

Just then she remembered that the cows in Farmer Brown's barnyard had no water to drink, so she said "Good-by" to Grandfather Frog and hurried away to turn the windmill that would pump the water for them.

Grandfather Frog sat on his big green lily pad and watched her go. "Now what can be the most beautiful thing in the whole world?" said Grandfather Frog to himself. He looked over the Smiling Pool. What could the old briar patch have more beautiful than the pure white water lilies smiling up at him? If the briar patch were not such a long way off, he would go see for himself. Just then he saw Billy Mink.

"Billy! Billy Mink!" called Grandfather Frog. "Old Mother West Wind says that she has just seen the most beautiful thing in the whole world, and it is over in the old briar patch."

"Huh!" cried Billy Mink. "There's nothing beautiful in that old briar patch!"

Now Billy Mink is naturally curious. The more he thought about the most beautiful thing in the whole world, the more he wanted to see it.

So presently he hitched up his trousers and started across

the Green Meadows towards the old briar patch. On the way he met Jimmy Skunk.

"Where are you going, Billy Mink?" asked Jimmy Skunk.

"Over to the old briar patch to see the most beautiful thing in the whole world," replied Billy Mink.

"I'll go with you," said Jimmy Skunk, for he had had a good breakfast of fat beetles and had nothing special to do.

So, one behind the other, Billy Mink and Jimmy Skunk trotted along the Lone Little Path across the Green Meadows. Pretty soon they met Johnny Chuck.

"Where are you going?" asked Johnny Chuck.

Billy Mink and Jimmy Skunk looked a wee bit foolish. "We're going to see the most beautiful thing in the whole world," said Billy Mink and Jimmy Skunk together.

"Where is it?" asked Johnny Chuck.

"Over in the old briar patch," replied Billy Mink.

"I'll go with you," said Johnny Chuck.

So the three, one behind the other, trotted along the Lone Little Path across the Green Meadows. As they passed the big hickory tree, Sammy Jay saw them.

"Where are you going?" called Sammy Jay.

"To see the most beautiful thing in the whole world," replied Billy Mink and Jimmy Skunk and Johnny Chuck, and

trotted on along the Lone Little Path across the Green Meadows.

Sammy Jay scratched his head. "Now what can there be more beautiful than this blue coat of mine?" said Sammy Jay, for you know he is very vain, oh, very vain indeed. The more he thought about it, the more sure he was that there could be nothing more beautiful than his handsome coat. But if there was — Sammy Jay flirted his tail and started to follow Billy Mink, Jimmy Skunk, and Johnny Chuck.

Halfway across the Green Meadows they met Bobby Coon and Happy Jack Squirrel.

"Where are you going?" asked Bobby Coon.

"Over to the old briar patch to see the most beautiful thing in the whole world," replied Billy Mink. "Come along with us."

"No," replied Bobby Coon. "I'm too sleepy." You see Bobby Coon had been out all night and he could hardly keep his eyes open.

But Happy Jack Squirrel said he would go; so the four, Billy Mink, Jimmy Skunk, Johnny Chuck, and Happy Jack Squirrel, one behind the other, trotted along the Lone Little Path across the Green Meadows, and behind them flew Sammy Jay. Presently they came to the old briar patch. It looked just as it had always looked, which really wasn't beau-

tiful at all. It was a great, tangled mass of brambles, with ugly-looking thorns sticking out in all directions. Billy Mink stepped on a thorn.

"Ouch!" cried Billy Mink.

Jimmy Skunk tried to crawl through between two bramble bushes and scratched his nose.

"Ouch!" cried Jimmy Skunk.

Johnny Chuck put his head through a little opening, and the briars pricked his ears.

"Ouch!" cried Johnny Chuck.

A crafty old bramble caught in Happy Jack Squirrel's tail.

"Ouch!" cried Happy Jack.

Then from the middle of the old briar patch they heard a voice. It was Peter Rabbit's voice.

"What are you looking for?" asked Peter Rabbit.

Peeping between the brambles, they saw Peter Rabbit in one of his secret hiding places. He had a little bundle of clover leaves and was picking out the sweetest and tenderest and feeding them to his little baby brother.

"We are looking for the most beautiful thing in the whole world," said Billy Mink. "Have you seen it, Peter Rabbit?"

"No," said Peter Rabbit, "I haven't seen the most beautiful thing in the whole world. What is it?"

"We don't know," replied Billy Mink. "But Old Mother West Wind said she saw it in the old briar patch. Come help us find it."

Peter Rabbit sat up for a minute, for Peter has a great deal of curiosity, a very great deal indeed. He wanted, oh, so much, to join the others and look for the most beautiful thing in the whole world. Then he looked down at his little baby brother, who was still hungry.

"I'll come pretty soon," said Peter Rabbit, and once more began to feed sweet, tender, young clover leaves to his little baby brother. He was hungry himself, but he would not touch a leaf until his baby brother had had enough, and, oh dear, that wasn't until the very last leaf had disappeared down his funny little throat.

Then Peter Rabbit started to try and find the most beautiful thing in the whole world. He hunted through all his secret little paths and hiding places in the briar patch, while the others hunted outside. They looked here, they looked there, they looked everywhere, but nowhere could they see the most beautiful thing in the whole world. Finally they gave it up.

Late that afternoon Grandfather Frog saw Billy Mink sitting on the Big Rock nursing the foot with which he had stepped on the thorn.

"Ho, Billy Mink!" called Grandfather Frog. "Did you find the most beautiful thing in the whole world?"

"No," said Billy Mink shortly. "It wasn't in the old briar patch. There was nothing and nobody there but Peter Rabbit feeding sweet, tender, young clover leaves to his little baby brother. The briar patch is the ugliest place in the whole world."

Grandfather Frog smiled to himself as he watched Billy Mink limp away to the Laughing Brook. He thought of Peter Rabbit feeding all his tender young clover leaves to his baby brother and he smiled again.

"Chugarum!" said wise old Grandfather Frog. "Old Mother West Wind was right. She did see the most beautiful thing in the whole world right there in the old briar patch, and Billy Mink saw it but didn't know it. And Jimmy Skunk saw it, and Johnny Chuck saw it, and Happy Jack saw it, and Sammy Jay saw it, yet not one of them knew it. They saw it when they watched Peter Rabbit feed all his sweet clover leaves to his little baby brother, and it is called 'love.'"

Old Mrs. Possum's Big Pocket

8

Unc' Billy Possum came proudly down the Lone Little Path through the Green Forest towards the big hollow tree which he had made his home. Peter Rabbit was the first to see him coming. Peter hurried to meet him, for Peter had prepared a surprise party to greet Unc' Billy and his family, for whom Unc' Billy had sent a short time before.

When Unc' Billy Possum saw all the little meadow and forest people gathered there to greet him and all the good things they had brought to eat, he was as surprised as Peter had hoped he would be. But Unc' Billy didn't show it! Oh, my, no! Unc' Billy never lets on that he is surprised at anything; he just grinned and grinned as only Unc' Billy Possum can grin.

"What yo' alls doin' at mah hollow tree?" demanded Unc' Billy, grinning more broadly than ever.

"It's a surprise party for you and your family," said Peter Rabbit. "We thought that Mrs. Possum and the children would be hungry, so everyone has brought something to eat. We want you to know how much we think of you and how glad we are that you are going to stay here in the Green Forest. I hope you will like the surprise party."

Unc' Billy made a very low bow. "Ah certainly am obliged to yo' alls for sech a right smart welcome to mah family," said Unc' Billy. "Ah reckons we alls are going to stay right here in the Green Forest, because yo' alls have made it so pleasant."

Now all this time everyone had been looking for Unc' Billy's family, and Danny Meadow Mouse could hold his curiosity in no longer.

"But where is your family, Unc' Billy?" he interrupted.

Unc' Billy grinned even more broadly than he had before. "Ah done left 'em back a piece, so as to see if the way was clear. Ah'll go and fetch 'em."

So Unc' Billy Possum started off up the Lone Little Path,

hurrying as fast as he could go, and everybody gathered close
around his hollow tree and watched to see his family arrive.
Pretty soon they saw him coming back down the Lone Little
Path, and behind him came old Mrs. Possum. She looked so
much like Unc' Billy that Johnny Chuck giggled right out
loud. Her own was just as thin and just as worn and just as
rumpled as Unc' Billy's old suit. Her face was just as sharp

and just as crafty as Unc' Billy's. But while Unc' Billy was grinning, old Mrs. Possum had never a smile; in fact, Mrs. Possum looked cross. She looked so cross that Peter Rabbit forgot all the nice things he had planned to say to her. You see, old Mrs. Possum had had a long journey, for she had come all the way from "ol' Virginny" and she was tired. The fact is, old Mrs. Possum had not wanted to come at all.

Now everyone had thought that Unc' Billy Possum had a big family, and when they saw no one but old Mrs. Possum, they didn't know what to make of it. But everyone was too polite to ask any questions. Each one came up in turn and was introduced by Unc' Billy. Mrs. Possum just grunted to each one until Jimmy Skunk came along.

Jimmy Skunk brought with him a big goose egg and offered it to Mrs. Possum with a very low bow. There is nothing in the world that Mrs. Possum likes better than fresh eggs, and this big goose egg made her smile in spite of herself. She just couldn't help it.

"It's fresh, and there are more where that came from," said Jimmy Skunk. "I certainly do hope you will like the Green Forest, Mrs. Possum. May I ask where your family is?"

Old Mrs. Possum's smile broadened into a grin just like Unc' Billy's, and her sharp little eyes twinkled.

"Certainly, Suh; they are in my pocket," said she.

When Mrs. Possum said this no one knew what to do or what to say. Who ever heard of carrying a family in a pocket? Old Mother West Wind carries her family of Merry Little Breezes in a big bag, but a big bag and a pocket are very different things.

Peter Rabbit looked at Jumper the Hare, and Jumper the Hare looked at Johnny Chuck, and Johnny Chuck looked at Jimmy Skunk, and Jimmy Skunk looked at Billy Mink, and Billy Mink looked at Jerry Muskrat, and Jerry Muskrat looked at Little Joe Otter, and Little Joe Otter looked at Happy Jack Squirrel, and Happy Jack Squirrel looked at Danny Meadow Mouse, and Danny Meadow Mouse looked at old Mr. Toad, and old Mr. Toad looked at Grandfather Frog, and Grandfather Frog looked at Prickly Porky, and no one said a word. Unc' Billy Possum winked at old Mrs. Possum and both of them grinned.

Finally Peter Rabbit, whose curiosity always must be satisfied, found his tongue.

"Did — did — I understand you to say that you have brought your family in your pocket?" he asked hesitantly.

"Yo' certainly did, Brer Rabbit," replied old Mrs. Possum.

Everyone looked at everyone else, more puzzled than be-

fore. Finally Prickly Porky cleared his throat. "Have — have you got your pocket with you?"

It was such a foolish question that everybody laughed. Unc' Billy laughed harder than anyone else, unless it was old Mrs. Possum herself.

"Of course Ah brought mah pocket with me," said she. "Would yo' alls like to see mah family?"

"If you please," said Jimmy Skunk, who never forgets to be polite.

Old Mrs. Possum climbed up on a stump where all could see her. My, how they did crowd around! Then very slowly she opened the big pocket in her gown and began to call one name after another. As she called, out of that big pocket popped one head after another, until there were eight little heads sticking out of that big pocket, and every little head was the exact image of Unc' Billy Possum's.

For a few minutes no one could say a word. It was so surprising that everyone rubbed his eyes to make sure that he saw aright.

Then Peter Rabbit hopped up on a log and made a speech. It wasn't very much of a speech, but he told old Mrs. Possum how he had planned this surprise party, and how the surprise was really theirs and not hers. He finished by suggesting that it was time to eat. Then everybody brought out the good things which they had prepared, and all began to eat and talk at once.

Old Mrs. Possum soon made herself at home in the Green Forest and kept house for Unc' Billy in his big hollow tree.

And Unc' Billy Possum found that with so many mouths to fill, he had to keep hunting for something to eat most of the time.

It was about this time that Farmer Brown's boy began to be troubled. Every day, when he went to collect the eggs in the hen house, he found that someone had been before him. The eggs grew scarcer and scarcer and scarcer. He knew that Jimmy Skunk was not stealing them, because he had stopped up the only place where Jimmy Skunk could get in. He remembered how he had once found Unc' Billy Possum in the hen house and he suspected that Unc' Billy was stealing the eggs now, though how he got in he did not know.

The more he thought about it, the more puzzled Farmer Brown's boy became. If Unc' Billy Possum was stealing the eggs, he must have a tremendous appetite to eat all of them. Finally he decided that he would go searching through the Green Forest and see if he could find Unc' Billy's home. So he shouldered his gun and called Bowser the Hound, and together they started down the Lone Little Path into the Green Forest.

Pretty soon Bowser the Hound began to sniff and sniff and sniff among the leaves.

"Bow-wow," said Bowser the Hound. Then he sniffed

some more, and all of a sudden he roared with all his big voice: "Bow-wow-wow-wow-wow!" Off he started as fast as he could run. Farmer Brown's boy had hard work to keep up with him. Bowser the Hound had found the trail of Unc' Billy Possum.

Now, Unc' Billy had been off hunting his breakfast in one direction, while old Mrs. Possum, with her family in her pocket, had started off in another direction. But Unc' Billy had had hard hunting and he had walked and walked and walked all through the Green Forest until, without knowing it, he had come over into the very part of the Green Forest where old Mrs. Possum was hunting.

When Unc' Billy heard Bowser the Hound coming, he hurried to the nearest hollow tree and was soon safely hidden inside, where he chuckled to himself, as he heard Bowser's big voice barking at the foot.

Farmer Brown's boy hurried up, but when he saw the big hollow tree, he knew that Unc' Billy was safe. He sat down on a stump to try to think of some plan to get Unc' Billy out, and while he thought, Bowser went hunting to see what else he could find. Suddenly Bowser's big voice rang out again and Bowser certainly seemed very much excited. You see, he had run across the tracks of old Mrs. Possum.

Now, Mrs. Possum had someone else to think about besides herself, for she had her eight children, who had been playing about on the ground. When she heard Bowser the Hound, she knew that she must hurry to some place of safety, and the only place she could think of was the very same hollow tree in which Unc' Billy was hiding. Of course, she didn't know that Farmer Brown's boy was sitting right close to the foot of it, and Farmer Brown's boy didn't know that there was a Mrs. Possum in the Green Forest.

Suddenly he heard a rustling in the bushes, then right before his eyes, up the hollow tree, scrambled the funniest sight he had ever seen. At first he could not make out what it was. It looked for all the world like a whole lot of animals rolled into one. He was so surprised that he forgot all about shooting until it was too late.

What he really did see was old Mrs. Possum with her eight children clinging to her. There hadn't been time for them to get into her big pocket, so some of them had just wrapped their tails around her long tail, some of them were clinging tight to her back, and some of them were hanging on around her neck.

It was so funny that Farmer Brown's boy just sat down and laughed. Pretty soon his face grew sober. "I guess," said he slowly, "I know now where all of my eggs have gone to."

And safe in old Mrs. Possum's big pocket, eight little Possums could have told Farmer Brown's boy that he guessed right.

Why Peter Rabbit Wears a White Patch

9

The Merry Little Breezes of Old Mother West Wind had been tumbled out of her bag very early this morning. Indeed, they were hardly awake when Old Mother West Wind shook them out on the Green Meadows and hurried away to her day's work, for she knew it was to be a very busy day.

The Merry Little Breezes had watched her go. They saw the great windmill in Farmer Brown's barnyard begin to whirl as she passed. They saw the million little leaves of the Green Forest shake, until a million little drops of dew, like a million little diamonds, fell down to the earth. And then Old Mother West Wind disappeared on her way to the Great Ocean, there to blow the white-winged ships along their way all day long.

The Merry Little Breezes stretched themselves and then began to dance across the Green Meadows to kiss the buttercups and daisies and to waken the sleepy little meadow people, who hadn't got their nightcaps off yet. But no one wanted to play so early in the morning. No, Sir, no one wanted to play. You see everyone had something more important to do. They loved the Merry Little Breezes, but they just couldn't stop to play. Finally the Merry Little Breezes gave it up and just curled up among the grasses for a sun-nap. That is, all but one did. That one kept hopping up every few minutes to see if anyone was in sight who would be likely to play a little while.

By and by he saw Peter Rabbit coming down the Lone Little Path from the Green Forest on his way to the dear old briar patch on the Green Meadows. Peter looked sleepy. The truth is, Peter had been out all night, and he was on his way home.

Halfway down the Lone Little Path Peter stopped, and sitting up very straight, looked over towards the Smiling Pool. He could see Mr. Redwing flying round and round, this way and that way over the bulrushes. He could hear Mr. Redwing's voice, and it sounded as if Mr. Redwing was very much excited. The more Peter looked and listened, the more certain he became that something very important must have happened over in the bulrushes on the edge of the Smiling Pool.

Now curiosity is Peter Rabbit's besetting sin. Sleepy as he was, he just couldn't go home without first finding out what had happened over in the bulrushes. So away Peter started for the Smiling Pool, lipperty-lipperty-lip. Of course the Merry Little Breeze saw him go. Then the Merry Little Breeze waked all the other Merry Little Breezes, and away they all danced across the Green Meadows to the Smiling Pool and stole in among the bulrushes behind Peter Rabbit to see what he was about. They came up just in time to hear Peter say:

"Hello, Mr. Redwing! You seem very much excited this fine morning. What is it all about? Has anything happened?"

Mr. Redwing hovered right over Peter Rabbit.

> *"Tra-la-la-la-lee, cherokee, cherokee!*
> *I'm happy, oh, so happy! I am happy as can be!"*

sang Mr. Redwing, looking down at Peter, who was sitting very straight and looking up.

"You seem to be. But what is it all about? What is it that makes you so happy this morning, Mr. Redwing?" Peter asked.

"Tra-la-la-la-lee, cherokee, cherokee!
We've another speckled egg, and this one makes it three!"

carolled Mr. Redwing, and flew over to the nest in the bulrushes where Mrs. Redwing was fussing about in a very important manner.

"Pooh!" said Peter Rabbit. "Is that all? What a little thing to make such a fuss about. I think I'll pay my respects to Grandfather Frog and then I'll go home."

Peter yawned. Then he hopped out where he could see all over the Smiling Pool. There sat Grandfather Frog on his big green lily pad, just as usual.

"Good morning, Grandfather Frog!" said Peter Rabbit.

"Chugarum! Of course it's a good morning. Every morning is good," replied Grandfather Frog gruffly.

"Oh!" said Peter Rabbit, and then he couldn't think of another thing to say.

The Merry Little Breezes giggled, and Grandfather Frog looked over at them and very slowly winked. Then he rolled his big goggly eyes up and stared into the sky. Peter Rabbit looked up to see what Grandfather Frog was looking at so intently. There was Redtail the Hawk swinging round and round in great big circles, as if he were trying to bore his way right into the clouds. Peter didn't stop to watch.

"When ol' Mr. Hawk is a-riding in the sky,
Keep a-moving, keep a-moving, keep a-moving mighty spry!"

chanted Peter, and taking his own advice, off he went, lipperty-lipperty-lipperty-lip.

Grandfather Frog watched the white patch on the seat of Peter's pants bobbing through the rushes until finally Peter was out of sight.

"Did you ever hear how Peter Rabbit happens to always wear a white patch on the seat of his pants?" asked Grandfather Frog.

"No; do tell us," exclaimed the Merry Little Breezes of Old Mother West Wind.

Grandfather Frog snapped up a foolish green fly, smacked his lips, cleared his throat, and began:

"Once upon a time when the world was young, Old Mother Nature found she had her hands full. Yes, Sir, she certainly did have her hands full. Her family was so big that she couldn't keep an eye on each one all the time. Dear me, dear me, such a lot of trouble as Old Mother Nature did have in those days! And no one made her more trouble than Peter

Rabbit's grandfather a thousand times removed. Mr. Rabbit was always in mischief. He just naturally couldn't keep out of it. He just hopped out of one scrape right plumb into another.

"Seemed like Old Mother Nature was kept busy just straightening out trouble Mr. Rabbit had made. Even she wasn't always quite sure who had made it, and no one else suspected Mr. Rabbit at all. He wore a brown coat, just like the brown leaves, and when he ran he looked just like a little old bunch of leaves blowing along. So Mr. Rabbit used to creep up and listen to what others were saying, for he was just as curious as Peter Rabbit is now, and he used to play all kinds of tricks and never get caught, because of that little old brown suit of his.

"One day in the early spring, when gentle Sister South Wind had melted all the snow, excepting a little patch right under the window of Mr. Skunk's house, Mr. Rabbit came strolling along that way with nothing special on his mind. Mr. and Mrs. Skunk were having a little family talk, and Mr. Skunk was speaking some loud. Mr. Rabbit stopped. Then Mr. Rabbit grinned and sat right down on that bed of snow under Mr. Skunk's window, where he could hear every word.

"Mr. Rabbit had been a-sitting there some time, listening to things that were none of his business, when he happened to look up. There was Old Mother Nature coming through the woods. She hadn't seen him yet, and Mr. Rabbit didn't mean that she should. Off he ran as fast as he could through the brown leaves, chuckling to himself. But Mr. Rabbit had forgotten to brush off the seat of his pants, and of course they were all white with snow.

"Old Mother Nature's eyes are sharp, and so of course she saw that white spot bobbing through the bushes, saw it right away. Mr. Rabbit had to stop and tell what he had been doing to get the seat of his pants all white with snow, and he told the truth, for it's of no use to tell anything else to Old Mother Nature. She looked very stern and she opened her mouth to tell Mr. Rabbit what she thought of him, and just then she had an idea. She just marched Mr. Rabbit off and sewed a white patch on the seat of his pants. And after that, when Mr. Rabbit tried to run away from the mischief he got into, everyone knew who it was by the white patch on the seat of his pants.

"And from that day to this all of Mr. Rabbit's family have worn a white patch, and that is why Peter wears one now, and whenever he stops running, if it is only for a minute, sits down on it so that it cannot be seen," concluded Grandfather Frog.

"Thank you! Thank you, Grandfather Frog!" cried the Merry Little Breezes, and hurried to see who would be the first one to blow a big, fat, foolish green fly within reach of Grandfather Frog's big mouth.

Who Stole the Eggs of Mrs. Grouse

10

There was great excitement in the Green Forest and on the Green Meadows. The Merry Little Breezes of Old Mother West Wind brought the news. They got it from Mrs. Grouse herself. They had found her very early that morning, almost distracted with grief. She had lost her eggs. Yes, Sir, someone had stolen all her eggs, fifteen of them, and she was in despair! She knew that they were stolen by some one who lived in the Green Forest and not by Farmer Brown's boy, because he had not been in the Green Forest that afternoon. She had left the nest for only a few minutes so that she might get the cramps out of her legs. When she came back, not an egg was to be seen.

Peter Rabbit hurried to call on Mrs. Grouse as soon as he heard the news. She told the dreadful story all over again, and Peter was so sympathetic that when she cried he cried a little, too. Now Peter is sharp-eyed and all the time he was listening to Mrs. Grouse he was examining everything in sight. What he saw he kept to himself. Pretty soon he excused himself and started down to Johnny Chuck's house. He found Johnny Chuck very busy making a new path.

"Hello, Johnny Chuck! Have you heard about the eggs of Mrs. Grouse?" asked Peter.

"Sure," said Johnny Chuck. "The Merry Little Breezes were so full of it that they couldn't talk of anything else this morning. Who do you suppose did it?"

"I don't suppose; I know," replied Peter Rabbit.

Johnny Chuck grinned. "Look out, Peter, you'll know too much someday," said he, for Peter is famous for thinking that he knows everything.

"I tell you I do know!" exclaimed Peter indignantly.

"You mean you think you know," replied Johnny Chuck.

"No such thing! I tell you I know who stole those eggs!" Peter fairly shouted.

"Did you see the thief?" asked Johnny Chuck.

"No," replied Peter.

"Or the stolen eggs?" asked Johnny.

"No," replied Peter.

"Then how do you know who stole them?" demanded Johnny.

"Because I found his tracks; that's how!" said Peter.

"Well, who do you think the thief is?" asked Johnny.

Peter tiptoed up and whispered in one of Johnny's ears.

"I don't believe it!" said Johnny Chuck. "Jimmy Skunk wouldn't do such a mean trick as that."

"I tell you I saw his tracks right around the nest," replied Peter.

"I don't care if you did, he never — "

Johnny Chuck didn't finish, for there, coming down the Lone Little Path, was Jimmy Skunk himself, and on the front

of his coat was a yellow stain. It certainly looked very much like egg.

The news of what Jimmy Skunk had done, or what Peter Rabbit thought he had done, spread all over the Green Meadows and through the Green Forest. No one would have anything to do with Jimmy. When he met Peter Rabbit, Peter turned his back to him. When he met Johnny Chuck, Johnny didn't see him. When he met Sammy Jay, Sammy yelled at the top of his lungs: "Thief! Thief! Thief!" It took Jimmy a long time to get it through his head that they really thought him a thief, and when he did realize it, he didn't know what they thought he had stolen. He couldn't very well ask, for no one would speak to him.

Jimmy Skunk lost his appetite. A beetle could run right under Jimmy's nose, and he would never know it. He grew thin. The more he worried, the thinner he grew. And he grew cross and short-tempered. Why, even little Danny Meadow Mouse turned up his nose when Jimmy passed, and Jimmy knew it.

Jimmy's thoughts were anything but pleasant thoughts as one day he started down the Crooked Little Path to the Green Meadows. Jimmy is naturally a lazy, good-natured, happy little fellow, and ready to make friends with anyone. This treatment he was receiving was more than he could bear. "If I only knew what it is all about!" he muttered to himself.

Just then he heard some voices over behind a bush and he thought he heard his own name. He stopped to listen. Of course this wasn't a nice thing to do, but when Jimmy heard his own name, he just had to try to hear more.

"I tell you I saw his tracks all around the nest of Mrs. Grouse, and I saw egg stain on the front of his coat!" It was Peter Rabbit who was speaking.

A great light broke over Jimmy Skunk. So that was what the matter was, and why they turned their backs on him and called him a thief! They thought that he was the one who had stolen the eggs of Mrs. Grouse! What right had they to think it? Jimmy grew indignant. Then he thought of what he had heard Peter Rabbit say. Jimmy gave a long whistle and sat down to think.

It certainly did look bad. He had been around the nest the very morning that the eggs were stolen. He remembered looking for beetles under an old log right back of where Mrs. Grouse had been sitting. And he *had* spilled egg on his coat, and then been in such a hurry to get home that he had not taken time to wash it off. But the egg came from Farmer Brown's hen house.

"I guess I don't blame them much, after all," said Jimmy, as he thought it all over. "And I guess that the only way I can prove it wasn't me is to find out who it was."

Now that Jimmy knew what the trouble was, he made up his mind that he would just turn policeman and find out who really did steal the eggs. He sat down to think it all over.

"Peter Rabbit doesn't eat eggs, and neither does Johnny Chuck," said Jimmy. "Danny Meadow Mouse might eat a wee, wee one, but he never could have stolen all those of Mrs. Grouse. Goodness, no!" Jimmy laughed at the thought. "Striped Chipmunk couldn't have done it, and Chatterer the Red Squirrel couldn't have kept still about it. It might have been Billy Mink or — " Jimmy Skunk drew a long breath and then he sprang to his feet. "I believe that that is just who it is!" he exclaimed.

Now Jimmy Skunk naturally is lazy, but this time he acted promptly. He brushed his coat carefully, and made himself as fine as he could.

Then he started out to make some calls. He first stopped at Johnny Chuck's house, but Johnny had seen him coming, and when Jimmy knocked, Johnny pretended that he wasn't at home. Jimmy grinned and went on. At almost every house he was treated in just the same way. When he had called, or tried to call, on most of the little people of the Green Meadows and the Green Forest, he had made up his mind that none of these was the thief, for it was plain to see that they all held him guilty.

Jimmy chuckled to himself as he thought over the way he had been received. "Well, anyway, I know now who it wasn't, and that is something; now to find out who it was!" said he, as he started for the Laughing Brook.

Coming down the Laughing Brook from the Smiling Pool he met Billy Mink. Billy had a fat trout which he was taking home. He laid it down to say "howdy" to Jimmy Skunk, for Billy Mink is so often in mischief that he cannot afford to turn his back on others. Besides, he is a sort of second cousin to Jimmy Skunk.

"Howdy," said Jimmy Skunk. "I suppose that your store-house is full of fat trout, Billy Mink."

Billy scowled. "It was," he replied, "but that thieving cousin of ours, Shadow the Weasel, stole from it yesterday. I caught him, and I guess he wishes now that he hadn't. He isn't smart enough to catch his own fish, so he steals from his own cousins."

"I thought Shadow the Weasel had gone on a long journey," said Jimmy.

"He's been back a week," replied Billy shortly. "Well, I must be going, good-by!"

"Good-by," replied Jimmy Skunk, and with a light heart he started back for the Crooked Little Path up the hill, for he had found out what he wanted to know — Shadow the Weasel was back in the Green Forest.

Jimmy went on to the top of the Crooked Little Path and then sat down to watch Old Mother West Wind gather her Merry Little Breezes into the big bag in which she would carry them to her home behind the Purple Hills. As he watched, Jimmy would sometimes look over towards Farmer Brown's and chuckle. He was waiting for the black shadows to creep out from the Purple Hills.

By and by he saw them coming, creeping slowly, slowly out across the Green Meadows and up the Crooked Little Path to his very feet. When it had grown quite dark, Jimmy Skunk arose and started for Farmer Brown's hen house. He knew just where every nest was, for he had been there many times before. In the second one he looked into was a nice brown egg. It made Jimmy's mouth water, for Jimmy is very fond of eggs. But he closed his lips tightly and picked up the egg. Then he crept out of the hen house and hurried, actually hurried, which is something very unusual for Jimmy Skunk, over to the Green Forest, where he hid the egg in a hollow stump. Then back he hurried for another egg. Three times he made the trip to Farmer Brown's hen house, and each time he brought back an egg to put in the hollow stump.

By this time Jimmy Skunk was tired. But he couldn't stop to rest now. Down to the Laughing Brook he hurried and there he found Billy Mink.

"Hi, Billy Mink! I want a fish," said Jimmy Skunk.

Billy Mink laughed. "Catch it then!" he cried.

"Come here; I want to whisper something," replied Jimmy Skunk.

Billy Mink came over and listened. Then he grinned. "All right," said he, "I'll do anything to get even with Shadow the Weasel."

So presently Billy Mink, who is a famous fisherman, brought Jimmy Skunk a fat fish, and Jimmy thanked him. Then he dragged it up through the Green Forest and finally put it in the hollow stump with the eggs. When he had done this, he hurried off to find Peter Rabbit and Johnny Chuck, for it was then just the beginning of the morning. It was hard work, but finally he got them to come up and hide with him near the hollow stump.

They had been there but a little while when they heard a

rustling of the leaves. Jimmy reached over and poked Peter Rabbit. There was Shadow the Weasel running with his nose to the ground and following the smell of fish where Jimmy Skunk had dragged the trout that Billy Mink had given him.

Straight up to the hollow stump went Shadow the Weasel. He peeped inside. Then he looked all around to see if anyone was watching. He didn't see Jimmy Skunk and Peter Rabbit and Johnny Chuck.

"My!" exclaimed Shadow the Weasel. "These are better than the eggs of Mrs. Grouse!" and he disappeared in the hollow stump.

Peter Rabbit looked at Jimmy Skunk. Then he held out his hand. "I'm sorry, Jimmy Skunk, that I ever thought that it was you who stole the eggs of Mrs. Grouse. Now I'm going to hurry to tell everyone on the Green Meadows and in the Green Forest who it really was."

And Peter was as good as his word, so that everyone hurried to tell Jimmy Skunk how much they thought of him.

How Digger the Badger Came to the Green Meadows

11

The little people who live down on the Green Meadows were beginning to feel envious of the little folks who dwell in the Green Forest. Yes, Sir, they were beginning to feel envious, and you know that envy is a very bad feeling to have. But somehow they couldn't seem to help it. And it was all because it seemed as if every stranger who arrived chose the Green Forest for his home instead of the beautiful, broad Green Meadows. There was Prickly Porky, who had come down from the North Woods. And there was Unc' Billy Possum, who had come up from way down in "ol' Virginny." And there was Ol' Mistah Buzzard, who had come up from the same place, so as to be neighbor to Unc' Billy. They all chose the Green Forest to live in. Johnny Chuck and Jimmy Skunk and Danny Meadow Mouse sat in Johnny Chuck's dooryard talking it over.

"It isn't fair!" said Johnny Chuck, carefully brushing sand from the seat of his trousers. "It just isn't fair."

Jimmy Skunk stretched himself out lazily and yawned. "That's right, Johnny Chuck, it isn't fair," said he. "Anyway, the Green Meadows are prettiest."

"Of course they are!" Danny Meadow Mouse broke in. "There isn't anything else in all the world so beautiful as the Green Meadows!"

Jimmy Skunk and Johnny Chuck laughed. Jimmy got up and stretched lazily and looked away across the Green Meadows to the Crooked Little Path that comes down the hill. He straightened up suddenly and shaded his eyes with his hands while he looked more closely.

"Who's that coming down the Crooked Little Path?" he exclaimed.

Johnny Chuck looked. It was nobody Johnny knew. All this time little Danny Meadow Mouse was trying his best to see, too, but he couldn't, because he is so little that even when he stretched himself up on the tips of his toes he couldn't see over the meadow grass.

"Climb up on my shoulders," said Johnny Chuck, who always is good-natured.

So Danny Meadow Mouse climbed up on the shoulders of Johnny Chuck. He looked over to the Crooked Little Path down the hill, and what he saw excited him so that he nearly fell off of Johnny Chuck's shoulders. It was a stranger, and he was coming right straight down onto the Green Meadows. Yes, Sir, there was no doubt about it! He was coming right straight down onto the Green Meadows without so much as a look at the Green Forest.

Nearer and nearer drew the stranger. He had short legs, very short legs. They were so short that as he moved along his legs could hardly be seen at all. And such stout legs! They were the stoutest legs that Johnny Chuck or Jimmy Skunk or Danny Meadow Mouse had ever seen. And the stranger was so broad that it was almost hard work to tell whether he was broadest or longest. He wore a long, silky, gray coat that hung down on each side. His waistcoat was light and he had the queerest sharp black and white face. He walked slowly, as if he had come a great way and was very, very tired. When he reached Johnny Chuck's dooryard he stopped.

"How do you do?" said Johnny Chuck in his most polite manner.

"Howdy," replied the stranger gruffly.

"Have you come far?" asked Jimmy Skunk.

The stranger sighed. "I should say I have! I've come all the way out of the Great West," replied the stranger.

Danny Meadow Mouse had edged off to a safe distance as the stranger approached. So many were always looking for Danny to gobble him up that he had no mind to run any risks with a total stranger. "May I ask who you are?" he called, in his funny, squeaky little voice.

"Sure, son!" was the reply. "I'm Digger the Badger. Everybody out in the Great West knows me."

"Are you going to stay here long?" asked Johnny Chuck.

"I don't know. I'm just looking for a home. Is this a good place to live?" inquired Digger the Badger.

"The best place in all the world!" cried Johnny Chuck and Jimmy Skunk and Danny Meadow Mouse together.

"Then this is just the place I want to live!" declared Digger. "I think I'll look around a bit."

So off he went this way and that over the Green Meadows, while Johnny Chuck and Jimmy Skunk and Danny Meadow Mouse excitedly wondered if this stranger really would make his home on the Green Meadows. Now it was getting late in the afternoon, and Digger the Badger was very, very tired, so finally he curled up under a little bush and went to sleep. And before he closed his eyes he had about made up his mind that he would stay and make his home on the Green Meadows.

When Digger the Badger crawled out from under the little bush the next morning, it was so early that no one was astir but Old Mother West Wind. Digger watched her come down from the Purple Hills and wondered and wondered what she could be carrying in the big bag over her shoulder. When she reached the middle of the Green Meadows she stopped, opened her big bag, turned it upside down, and shook it. Out tumbled all her children, the Merry Little Breezes, and began the merriest, funniest little dance among the buttercups and daisies.

And as they danced, they sang. Digger the Badger stopped brushing his clothes to listen, and as he listened he began to smile, for this is what he heard:

> *"We're the Merry Little Breezes*
> *And we love to romp and play.*
> *We're the Merry Little Breezes*
> *And we're happy all the day.*

"Oh, we love the pretty flowers,
And the little birds that sing,
And we love the sun and showers
Of the summer and the spring.

"So we play and romp together
From the dawn till day is thro',
But most of all we're happy
When there's some good deed to do."

"That settles it!" said Digger the Badger, right out loud. "That settles it! I'm going to make my home right here on the Green Meadows!"

"Is that so? Who invited you, I want to know?"

Digger whirled around. There sat Reddy Fox. Reddy had swelled himself up as big as he could, and every hair of his long red coat stood on end, so that he did look twice as big as he really is. He was trying hard to look very fierce, for you know Reddy is a bully. But all the time he took care, very great care not to come too near, for you know a bully is always a coward. Digger the Badger grinned.

"I reckon it isn't any of your business who invited me," said he. "I usually make my home where I please, and this

time I please to make it right here on the Green Meadows."

"You can't unless I say so," replied Reddy Fox, showing all his teeth. "There can't anyone come here to live unless I say so."

Digger the Badger didn't say a word. He just yawned. Yes, Sir, he yawned right in the face of Reddy Fox! And when he yawned, Reddy saw such long, strong teeth that he suddenly backed away just a little. Still he tried to appear very important and very fierce.

"You can't unless I say so!" he repeated.

Digger the Badger looked Reddy Fox straight in the face a whole minute without saying a word. Then, without any warning, he threw a whole handful of sand right in Reddy's face. "Bah!" shouted Digger the Badger.

What do you think Reddy did? Why, every hair dropped back into place, and without stopping to brush the sand out of his whiskers, he put his tail between his legs and sneaked away. And all the time Digger was laughing fit to kill himself.

"Now I am sure I will make my home on the Green Meadows," said Digger the Badger, and straightway began to dig.

And Johnny Chuck and Jimmy Skunk and Danny Meadow Mouse, watching from a distance, were no longer envious of the little folks who dwell in the Green Forest. And this is how Digger the Badger came to live on the Green Meadows.

Why Mistah Mocker Is the Best Loved of All the Birds

12

Mistah Mocker the Mockingbird had come up to the Green Forest to make his home there so as to be near his old neighbors, Unc' Billy Possum and Ol' Mistah Buzzard. They had come up from the sunny South a long time ago, and Mistah Mocker had missed them so much that now he had come up too. Unc' Billy Possum and Ol' Mistah Buzzard had made friends with all the little meadow and forest people right away. Indeed, they were thought a great deal of. You see they were always good-natured and always ready to tell a story about their old home "way down in ol' Virginny." So everybody, that is almost everybody, was very fond of Unc' Billy Possum and Ol' Mistah Buzzard. Reddy Fox wasn't, but

Reddy Fox isn't fond of anybody, excepting old Granny Fox.

But with Mistah Mocker the Mockingbird it was different. Yes, indeed, it was quite different. In the first place he was very independent and very proud. He just wouldn't ask favors of anybody. He would rather starve than beg. Oh, Mistah Mocker certainly was very independent. And then he was bashful, was Mistah Mocker. You see he didn't feel at home, and you know how it is when you don't feel at home. He just felt very uncomfortable and shy and out of place.

Now Mistah Mocker isn't much of a dresser. He doesn't care anything about fine clothes. He wears a modest gray suit trimmed with white, which he keeps in the best of order, but there isn't a thing about him to attract attention, excepting that he carries himself proudly, as becomes a member of one of the old families from way down South. When Sammy Jay first saw him, Sammy turned up his nose. You know Sammy Jay wears a very fine coat of bright blue trimmed with white, and is very proud of it. In fact, Sammy Jay thinks himself a very fine gentleman, though he seldom acts as a gentleman should.

"Pooh!" said Sammy Jay to Peter Rabbit. "If I didn't have a better looking suit than Mistah Mocker has, I wouldn't hold my head so high. He hasn't anything to be proud of!"

" 'Handsome is as handsome does,' you know, Sammy Jay. Have you heard Mistah Mocker sing?" asked Peter Rabbit.

"No," replied Sammy Jay, "and I don't want to. What does singing amount to, anyway?"

"A whole lot more than wearing fine clothes and screaming 'Thief! Thief!' when honest people are about!" said Bobby Coon, who happened along just in time to hear Sammy Jay.

Sammy Jay looked a wee bit foolish and uncomfortable. He was just about to make a sharp retort when Bobby Coon added:

"Ol' Mistah Buzzard says that Mistah Mocker is the best loved of all the birds way down South where he came from."

Peter Rabbit pricked up his long ears at once. Peter is very, very curious about other people's affairs and he dearly loves a story. He couldn't sit still now.

"Let's go right over now and ask Ol' Mistah Buzzard why it is that everybody down South is so fond of Mistah Mocker!" said Peter.

Sammy Jay and Bobby Coon having nothing better to do that morning, agreed. On the way they told Johnny Chuck and Happy Jack Squirrel and Striped Chipmunk and Jimmy Skunk and Danny Meadow Mouse and Billy Mink where they were going and what they were going for. Billy Mink hurried down to the Smiling Pool and told Little Joe Otter and Jerry Muskrat, and they hurried to catch up with the others. So it happened that when Ol' Mistah Buzzard grew tired of sailing round and round, way, far up in the blue, blue sky, and came down, down, down to his favorite roost on a tall dead tree in the Green Forest, he found quite a gathering of the little forest and meadow people waiting for him. Ol' Mistah Buzzard's eyes twinkled.

"Ah cert'nly am right proud to see yo' alls. What can Ah do fo' yo'?" said Ol' Mistah Buzzard.

Peter Rabbit hopped out in front and made a bow in his most polite manner.

"If you please," said he, "we would like to know why it is that your friend, Mistah Mocker, is the best loved of all the birds in the sunny South where you came from," said Peter.

Ol' Mistah Buzzard's eyes twinkled more than ever, as he settled himself comfortably and looked down on his little friends of the Green Forest and the Green Meadows.

"It isn't much of a story," said he.

"But we want to hear it! Please tell us just the same! Please do, Mistah Buzzard!" they all cried together.

So Ol' Mistah Buzzard drew a long breath, scratched his

bald head thoughtfully, cleared his throat, and began:

"Once upon a time a li'l', no 'count bird lived way down Souf where Mistah Jack Frost am plumb skeery of coming 'less he fergit how to pinch any mo'. He was jes' a plain, quiet li'l' bird, jes' the plainest, quietest li'l' bird ever was. He didn't pay any 'tention to what other folks were about, but went around from mo'ning till night 'tending to his own bus'ness right smart."

Ol' Mistah Buzzard looked very hard at Peter Rabbit as he said this. Peter turned his face away and looked just a little bit foolish and wriggled uneasily. But he didn't say anything, and after a few minutes Ol' Mistah Buzzard cleared his throat once more and began again.

"He wore ve'y plain clo'es, did this li'l', no 'count bird Ah been telling yo' about, and Mistah Redbird and Mistah Jaybird and some others who wore fine clo'es turned up their noses at him, and when they met him p'tended that they didn't see him no how."

When Mistah Buzzard said this he looked very hard at Sammy Jay, and of course everybody else looked very hard at Sammy Jay. But Sammy didn't seem to notice it. He was very busy fixing his light waistcoat so that it would set better. Ol' Mistah Buzzard just grinned. Then he went on with his story.

"But this li'l', no 'count bird went right 'long minding his own bus'ness, and befo' long it got so that nobody took any notice er him no mo' 'nif he wasn't 'round. When it come springtime, all the other birds began to get ready to go on a long journey, and they made a right smart fuss about it, same as mos' folks do. Fo' a week they did nothing but talk about the beautiful No'th they was going to, till yo' would have tho't the Souf, what had given 'em warmth and sunshine all winter long, was the meanest land on the face of the earth. And all the time they was a-talking, they was a-fixing their clo'es and a-fussing themselves all up fo' the long journey.

"But this li'l', no 'count bird Ah'm telling yo' about, he didn't have a word to say. No, Suh, he didn't have a word to say. He jes' kep' his tongue stuck in his cheek and went right along minding his own bus'ness jes' the same as ever. When the time came fo' the gran' start fo' the long journey to the No'th, and all the other birds rose up in the air, pushing and crowding like the sky wasn't big enuff to hold all er 'em, this li'l', no 'count bird jes' stayed behind and went right along minding his own affairs same as ever.

"Now of course, when all the other birds had gone, it grew right smart lonesome down there in the Souf. Yes, Suh, it cert'nly did grow lonesome! The pine trees kep' a-sighing and a-sighing. Ev'body went around a-listening and a-listening and a-listening. Because why? Because there were no sweet songs like there had been all winter. Ev'ywhere it was still and solemn, jes' like somebody was daid.

"Well, one mo'ning ev'ybody came rushing out of their houses, and ev'ybody was a-laughing and shouting and clapping their hands. What fo'? Because they tho't all the birds had come back to the Souf once more. The song of first one and then another and another and another came pouring out of the top of the tallest pine tree. Ev'ybody rushed over to the tallest pine tree and looked and looked, till it seemed like they would break their necks, but all they could see was jes' this plain, quiet, li'l', no 'count bird Ah'm telling yo' about.

"There he sat, right on the top of the tallest pine tree, jes' as plain and no 'count looking as ever. But ev'y time he opened his mouth there came pouring out from his li'l' throat such music as never befo' came out of one throat.

"There he sat on the top of the tallest pine tree, singing the songs of all the other birds what had flown away up No'th. Yes, Suh, that is jes' what he was doing, and he had the song of ev'y one of those other birds from the po' singers to the best.

"All winter long, while that li'l', no 'count bird had been going about his bus'ness, he had been a-listening and a-listening, and a-studying and a-studying the songs of all the other birds. Then he had gone off, way off deep in the woods, and there he had practiced and practiced until he could sing as well as the other birds and even better.

"So all summer long this li'l', no 'count bird sang and sang to keep the Soufland from getting lonesome, till in the fall the other birds came flocking back to get away from ol' Jack Frost. When they got there, what do yo' think they found? Why, they found that the li'l', no 'count bird that they had left behind in the spring was now the best loved of all, and that the Souf didn't really care whether they came back or not.

"And that li'l', no 'count bird Ah been telling yo' about

was the grandaddy a thousand times removed of mah friend, Mistah Mocker, who has come up to live in the Green Forest and on the Green Meadows, and because Mistah Mocker has got his grandaddy's voice, he is jes' as much loved in the Souf as his grandaddy was, and Ah hopes that yo' alls will love him just the same," concluded Ol' Mistah Buzzard.

"I'm sure we will, and thank you very much for the story, Mistah Buzzard," said Peter Rabbit. "Now let's all hunt up Mistah Mocker and ask him to sing for us!"

And that is just what they did.

The Impudence of Mr. Snake

13

Johnny Chuck was going down the Lone Little Path on his way to the sweet clover patch for his breakfast. Johnny was thinking of nothing in particular, and paying no attention to anything in particular. Suddenly he heard a gentle little hiss. Johnny Chuck stopped short right where he was. He knew that hiss as well as if he had been looking right at the maker of it. It was the hiss of Mr. Snake, but which Mr. Snake Johnny Chuck was not sure. If it was the hiss of little Mr. Gartersnake or little Mr. Greensnake, Johnny didn't care, but if it was the hiss of Mr. Copperhead, Johnny did care. It was to make sure who had hissed at him that Johnny Chuck had stopped so short.

"It is always best to be sure and safe," said Johnny Chuck, as his sharp little eyes looked this way and that way. Just before him, curled up in the Lone Little Path, was little Mr. Greensnake. He was sticking his tongue out at Johnny Chuck and trying to make himself look very fierce. Johnny Chuck laughed.

"You don't suppose that I am afraid of you, do you?" he cried.

Little Mr. Greensnake just hissed louder than ever and ran his tongue out at Johnny Chuck in the sauciest way. He didn't intend to move out of Johnny Chuck's way unless he had to.

Johnny Chuck looked at little Mr. Greensnake very hard, and little Mr. Greensnake ran his tongue out again. Johnny Chuck's temper began to rise, and so did the hair of his coat, until he looked almost twice as big as he really is. Little Mr. Greensnake didn't say anything, but he made up his mind that he had sudden and important business somewhere else and that he must be going right away. So without so much as begging Johnny Chuck's pardon, little Mr. Greensnake glided away through the grass, but as he went, he turned his head and once more stuck his tongue out at Johnny Chuck.

Johnny Chuck trotted on down the Lone Little Path, and as he trotted along, he began to think out loud. "I wonder what makes little Mr. Greensnake so very saucy," said he. "The idea of him sticking his tongue out at me that way for nothing! But now I think of it, little Mr. Gartersnake did the very same thing the last time I met him, and so did Mr. Adder and Mr. Copperhead and Mr. Blacksnake. I wonder if they stick their tongues out at everybody that way or if it's just at me."

"They stick them out at everybody, even at us. Isn't it dreadful?" said a soft little voice right in Johnny Chuck's ear. It was one of the Merry Little Breezes of Old Mother West Wind.

"I don't know," said the Merry Little Breeze. "I've seen Mr. Blacksnake stick his tongue out at Farmer Brown's boy, even when Farmer Brown's boy was trying to kill him with a stick. And when finally Mr. Blacksnake ran away, he kept turning and sticking his tongue out just the same. Did you ever hear of such impudence?"

Johnny Chuck shook his head. "I never did! I certainly never did!" he said. "Perhaps that is one reason why nobody likes them."

"I tell you what, let's go over to the Smiling Pool and ask Grandfather Frog if he knows why all the Snake family are so impudent," cried the Merry Little Breeze.

"The very thing!" cried the other Merry Little Breezes,

who had gathered around. "Grandfather Frog will be sure to know, for he is so very old and very wise. Come on, Johnny Chuck!"

Away raced the Merry Little Breezes across the Green Meadows to the Smiling Pool. Johnny Chuck started after them. But he is round and fat and roly-poly, and to run makes him huff and puff. Pretty soon he stopped and looked over to the Smiling Pool. The Merry Little Breezes were already there, as Johnny Chuck could tell by the way the bulrushes were nodding.

"I think that sweet clover will do me more good than one of Grandfather Frog's stories, which may or may not be true," said Johnny Chuck. "Besides, the Merry Little Breezes will tell me all about it if I tease them to, and then I'll have both the clover and the story."

So Johnny Chuck went on to the sweet clover patch and ate and ate and ate while the Merry Little Breezes were busy blowing fat, foolish, green flies within reach of Grandfather Frog's big mouth, for they knew that when he had enough fat, foolish, green flies inside his white and yellow waistcoat, Grandfather Frog is almost sure to feel good-natured, very good-natured indeed, and that is the time to beg a story. While they were hunting for fat, foolish, green flies, whom should they find but Mr. Blacksnake curled up on the bank of the Smiling Pool. Whenever they passed, he ran his tongue out at them.

When Grandfather Frog said that he couldn't tuck another fat, foolish, green fly inside his white and yellow waistcoat to save him, the Merry Little Breezes begged him for a story.

"Chugarum! What shall I tell you about?" asked Grandfather Frog.

The Merry Little Breezes pointed across the Smiling Pool to the bank where Mr. Blacksnake lay. "Tell us why he and all his relations stick their tongues out at all who pass," cried the Merry Little Breezes.

Old Grandfather Frog sat on his big, green lily pad and looked across at the sunny spot on the bank of the Smiling Pool. There lay Mr. Blacksnake taking a sunbath. Every time one of the Merry Little Breezes raced by him, or Bossy the Cow came near him, Mr. Blacksnake raised his head and stuck out his tongue. Yes, Sir, Mr. Blacksnake would run his tongue out at everyone who passed.

"Chugarum!" said Grandfather Frog. "That's what comes of impudence."

Grandfather Frog settled himself and pulled down his white and yellow waistcoat. Then he gazed again at the sunny bank where Mr. Blacksnake lay, and somehow it seemed to the Merry Little Breezes that Grandfather Frog wasn't looking at the sunny spot on the bank or at Mr. Blacksnake at all, but was looking way, way off. And so he was. He was looking into the days when the world was young. Presently he began to talk just as if he had forgotten all about the Merry Little Breezes and was talking to himself. The Merry Little Breezes drew close around him and settled down very still, very still indeed, for Grandfather Frog had begun a story.

"It happened a long time ago," said Grandfather Frog, "a very long time ago, in the days when the world was young. In those days the Snake family was a very important family. Yes indeed, a very important family. Old Mr. Snake, who wasn't old then, and was the head of the family, certainly was smart! Yes, Sir, old Mr. Snake certainly was smart! He was so smart that by and by people began to be afraid to do business with him, for somehow no one ever got the best of him. He always wore a handsome suit and he was extremely polite to everyone he met. 'Politeness don't cost anything,' old Mr. Snake used to say, and he certainly was free with his politeness and fine manners.

"What with his smart dress and his fine ways, people who had business with him couldn't think of anything but what a fine fellow Mr. Snake was, and all the time old Mr. Snake would be cheating them right and left. So Mr. Snake and all his family grew very rich; and the richer they grew, the more powerful they became; and the more powerful they became, the more polite was old Mr. Snake to everyone, rich and poor, high and low.

"Then one day along came Old Mother Nature to see how things were getting along, and to hear all complaints. Of course she saw right away how rich and powerful old Mr. Snake and his family had become, and how poor most of the other people had become. They all complained of hard times, hard times, but no one said a word against old Mr. Snake. Finally old Mr. Snake came to pay his respects to Old Mother Nature, and you may be sure that he was dressed in his best suit and brought his finest manners.

"Old Mother Nature began to ask him questions about how he came to be so rich, he and all his family, when all the others were crying hard times. Old Mr. Snake had an answer ready for every question, for his wit was quick and his tongue was smooth and oily, and all the time he was polite, oh, very polite. Not once did Old Mother Nature catch him with her sharp questions.

"Finally along came someone to speak to Old Mother

Nature, and she turned her back. Old Mr. Snake was so tickled to think how smart he had been in answering all her questions that for a minute he forgot all his politeness. What do you think he did? Why, he ran out his tongue at Old Mother Nature behind her back. Now with all his smartness, old Mr. Snake had not noticed a little pool of water in front of Old Mother Nature, in which she could see just what he was doing. Of course she saw him run his tongue out.

"What did she do? Why, from that day to this, all the Snake family have been compelled to run their tongues out at everyone they meet, so of course no one will have anything to do with such impudence — and they haven't a friend in the world," concluded Grandfather Frog.

Peter Rabbit's First Snow

14

Peter Rabbit pinched himself. Yes, Sir, that is just what Peter Rabbit did — pinched himself. Then he rubbed his eyes, and after that he pinched himself again. You see Peter wanted to be sure, really sure, that he was awake, and he was finding it very hard to be sure. Where were the Green Meadows and the Green Forest? They had disappeared all in a single night. Peter looked this way and looked that way, and his big eyes grew bigger with wonder. He couldn't see a single thing that looked as it had looked the night before. He knew that he was in his safe retreat in the middle of the dear old briar patch, for right over his head were friendly old brambles under which Peter had sat and dreamed often and often. And yet they had changed, and the old briar patch had become a new and beautiful place. The ground was covered with a carpet of white as soft as the down on Mrs. Quack's breast, and every smallest, teeniest, weeniest twig of the bushes growing among the brambles, and the brambles themselves, were piled high with this same soft white stuff, until they bent over to the ground and made the most wonderful caves and hiding places. It was a new world, a fairy world. Peter looked up in the blue, blue sky, and when he saw jolly, round, red Mr. Sun looking down and laughing at him just as usual, he gave a great sigh.

"It *is* real! It really *is* real! I wonder how it looks outside the old briar patch," he said, and started to find out.

How soft that white carpet was! Peter's feet sank into it as he hopped along one of his private little paths, which now stretched before him like a little white ribbon. Every time his feet sank in, he had a funny feeling. You see, this was the first time he had ever felt anything quite so soft and cool.

"What is it, anyway?" said Peter, talking to himself out loud. Then into his head popped some stories which he had heard old Mrs. Rabbit tell, when he was very, very small. "Why, this must be snow, and winter has really come!" cried Peter, suddenly sitting up very straight and clapping his hands. Then he kicked up his heels and scampered out on the

Green Meadows — only they were not green any more, but white, so beautifully white! And they sparkled so that Peter's eyes almost smarted from looking at them.

Peter looked back at the old briar patch, and then for the first time he saw something new — his own tracks. There they were, the print of each foot as plain as plain could be. It tickled Peter a lot to see them. He ran about to make more, running in circles and twisting and turning, and every few minutes sitting up to look at the funny patterns he had made in the snow. Then he kicked up his heels some more and did foolish things just because the world was so beautiful and he felt so happy.

"My!" said Peter to himself. "Just think of all that Johnny Chuck is missing by sleeping all winter! Why, I wouldn't have missed this for anything!"

You see this was Peter's first snow and first winter.

He felt as if he were living in a new world, a wonderful new world, a great white world of which he knew nothing at all. It was all very delightful and very strange. Peter jumped up and kicked his heels for very joy.

"There was an old lady lived up in the clouds,
A fussy old lady, 'twas plain to be seen.

She sputtered about and she puttered around,
A-rubbing and scrubbing to keep her house clean.

"Along came a rogue by the name of Jack Frost
And found this old lady's bed made up with care;
He opened the ticking, the feathers tossed out,
And people below said: 'There's snow in the air!' "

So sang Peter Rabbit, as he scampered across the snowy Green Meadows to the Green Forest, which was also white. There was the Lone Little Path, as plain as plain could be. Peter had to stop and stare at it because it was so plain. He remembered that in the summer, when the million little leaves had covered the bushes, the Lone Little Path had sometimes been very hard to see.

When Peter reached the big hollow tree where Unc' Billy Possum lives, there were no footprints in the snow around it, and so Peter knew that no one had been out that morning. He called and called, but no one answered.

"Pooh!" exclaimed Peter. "Must be everyone's asleep in there! Just think of what they are missing!"

Then he started off again, for he just felt that he had got to look into every one of the wonderful caves of snow under the hemlock trees. It was great fun. Here he was, right in the midst of the Green Forest he knew so well, and yet here on every side were strange white caves that he had never seen before, and odd mounds of sparkling white that puzzled Peter, until he found some familiar old stump or log hidden away underneath.

So Peter made his funny tracks all through the Green Forest, until finally he grew just a wee bit tired and sat down in one of the white caves to rest.

"How still, how very still it is!" thought Peter. Not a sound could he hear. He began to have just a wee bit of lonely feeling. It was great fun exploring this new world, but he wanted to talk it all over with someone. Could it be that everybody but himself had gone to sleep for all winter? What a dreadful thought! But just as Peter began to be afraid that this was really true, he heard a voice way over near the Laughing Brook, and the voice cried: "Thief! Thief! Thief!"

Then he heard another voice sputtering and scolding so fast that the words seemed to just fall over each other. Peter smiled. "Sammy Jay and Chatterer the Red Squirrel wouldn't be happy, not even in such a beautiful world as this, without quarreling," said he, as he hopped off in the direction of the Laughing Brook.

Sammy Jay and Chatterer the Red Squirrel were calling

each other names as fast as their tongues could go. It was good to hear them. Yes, Sir, those angry voices actually sounded good to Peter Rabbit, and he laughed aloud and ran faster. You see Peter had begun to think that he was the only one awake in that wonderful great white fairy world. That is why the quarreling voices of Sammy Jay and Chatterer sounded so good to him. Besides, he knew that their quarrels never amount to anything, and that it is really their way of enjoying themselves.

> A pointed tongue has Sammy Jay
>   And Chatterer has sharpened wits;
> Now tell us, pray, if you can see
>   How gentle speech with either fits.

It doesn't, and both Sammy Jay and Chatterer the Red Squirrel say a great many sharp things without really meaning them at all. When Peter came in sight, they stopped quarreling.

"Hello, Long Ears! I heard that you were going to sleep all winter," shouted Sammy Jay.

Peter grinned good-naturedly and made a face at Sammy Jay and Chatterer.

"Isn't it a great day?" he cried.

138

"Great!" replied Chatterer. "Have you got your snow-shoes on?"

"What are snowshoes?" asked Peter, pricking up his ears.

"Go ask Mrs. Grouse," replied Chatterer. "She has hers on this morning."

"Where is she?" asked Peter, preparing to start right away, for his curiosity would not let him sit still.

"Under the hemlocks up on the hill," replied Chatterer. "What's your hurry?"

But Peter was already on his way up the hill. Pretty soon he noticed some queer tracks in the snow. He had never seen any like them before. They looked just a little like the prints

of Mrs. Quack's feet, which he had once seen in the mud on the edge of Farmer Brown's duck pond. But Mrs. Quack never comes into the Green Forest; at least Peter never had seen her there. So Peter wondered and wondered whose tracks these could be and followed them to find out, forgetting all about Mrs. Grouse and her snowshoes.

Lipperty-lipperty-lip scampered Peter Rabbit, following the queer tracks. Indeed, he didn't have eyes for anything else, and almost ran plump into Mrs. Grouse herself.

"Haven't you anything better to do than to be running people down? Where are your eyes, Peter Rabbit?" snapped Mrs. Grouse, ruffling up her feathers.

"I — I beg your pardon!" said Peter. "There's a stranger in the Green Forest making queer tracks and — " Peter stopped and stared. Mrs. Grouse had walked away from him, and *she* was making the queer tracks.

"Ha, ha, ha!" laughed Mrs. Grouse. "I made them myself with my new snowshoes."

Peter looked at her feet. Sure enough, she was wearing snowshoes. They were of feathers which grew out between her toes, and when she walked on the snow she hardly sank in at all.

"My, I wish I had snowshoes!" cried Peter.

Mrs. Grouse Goes to Bed

15

Mrs. Grouse is somewhat particular as to where she sleeps. She has reason to be, has Mrs. Grouse, for there are old Granny Fox and Reddy Fox and Shadow the Weasel, not to mention Jimmy Skunk and Billy Mink, all of whom are much given to roaming through the Green Forest at night instead of sleeping, as Mrs. Grouse insists honest folks should. And there is Hooty the Owl, whose fierce hunting cry often and often wakens Mrs. Grouse from pleasant dreams to shiver for a minute. She knows that there is not one of them but would be glad of a meal of plump grouse. By daylight she has no fear of them. Then her strong, swift wings will carry her to safety in the twinkling of an eye. They know it,

too, and by daylight are always quite polite to Mrs. Grouse.

So Mrs. Grouse is a little bit fussy as to where she sleeps. There is a certain big hemlock tree whose great green branches made the snuggest of friendly hiding places, and in this for a long time Mrs. Grouse had tucked her head under her wing every night; nobody knew anything about it, for always before she flew up there she made very sure that no one was about to see her. But Mrs. Grouse prefers to be on the ground, and if she had felt at all safe, she would rather have slept on the ground than in the friendly hemlock tree. Sometimes, when fierce Mr. North Wind blows, she shivers a little in spite of her warm cloak of feathers.

There came a day when down through the bare branches of the Green Forest sifted a million little snowflakes. Mrs. Grouse watched them pile up and pile up a great soft blanket on the ground, and she smiled as she watched, for Mrs. Grouse had a plan, the most splendid plan, for a good night's rest. The black shadows came creeping through the Green Forest very early that day, and Mrs. Grouse sat on a branch of the hemlock tree, smiling and watching the million little snowflakes sifting down and sifting down. Just before it became really dark, she took a good look all about, to be sure that no one was watching, and then — what do you think she did? Why, she just dived head first down into the deepest, softest pile of snow and worked her way along for several feet. Then she turned around two or three times, fluffed out her feathers, made herself very comfortable and tucked her head under her wing.

> "I love the gentle snow that falls
>   And turns the world all white;
> It makes the very nicest bed,
>   With blanket soft and light.

> "Though Hooty's eyes are big and round
>   He cannot see me here;
> From Granny Fox and Jimmy Skunk
>   I've not a thing to fear.

> "Jack Frost may blow his coldest blast,
>   The storm rage high and low,
> I do not care the least, wee bit,
>   Down here beneath the snow."

Almost before she had finished saying this, Mrs. Grouse was fast asleep. The snowflakes sifted down and filled up the hole that Mrs. Grouse had made when she plunged into the snow. Late that night it stopped snowing, and the moon came out.

Then Granny Fox and Reddy Fox started out to hunt, for they were hungry. They came down from the faraway Old Pasture to the Green Forest. It was hard work wading through the snow, and by and by they sat down to rest. Though they didn't know it, they were almost over Mrs. Grouse, who was dreaming of warm spring days.

"Ugh! I don't like snow! It tires me all out to walk through it, and it covers up things so! I haven't smelled a single track since we left the Old Pasture. I say, let's go to Farmer Brown's hen house; I'm dreadfully hungry," whined Reddy Fox.

Old Granny Fox looked at Reddy out of the corner of one eye. "You're young and I'm old," said she, "and you ought to be able to stand a lot more than I can. I'm hungry, too, but I'm not hungry enough yet to be willing to risk my skin by going up to Farmer Brown's hen house. An empty stomach is a whole lot better than a skin full of shot. I should think that you would have learned that by this time. I was going to propose that we take up our old home here on the edge of the Green Meadows again, but if you are still such a foolish young fox as to talk of going to Farmer Brown's hen house the very first time you feel emptiness in your stom-

ach, I guess we'd better stay up in the Old Pasture. There isn't much to eat there in winter, and you'll have the hardest hunting you've ever had, but you'll be safe."

Reddy hung his head. He was ashamed of having complained. He knew that what Granny Fox said was true. He tried hard not to think that he was hungry, but inside was such an emptiness, such a dreadful emptiness, that it was hard work to think of anything else. And when he thought of Farmer Brown's hen house, with its roosts full of sleeping hens, it seemed as if he just had to go up there.

"One hen wouldn't be missed," muttered Reddy.

Old Granny Fox turned and cuffed Reddy's ears. "I used to think that you had some fox sense in that head of yours, but you haven't got even common sense," she snapped. "Look behind you at those tracks. Don't you suppose Farmer Brown's boy has got eyes in his head? When he came out to feed the hens in the morning, the very first thing that he would see would be your tracks, and you couldn't cover them up the way you can on bare ground. Now don't let me hear any more of this nonsense!"

Reddy looked back at the tracks he and Granny had made, and for the first time he realized what a telltale the snow is and he hated it more than ever.

"You're right, Granny Fox, just as you always are, and I'll try not to even think of Farmer Brown's hen house," said he meekly.

Granny grinned as she said:

> "*An empty stomach sharpens wit;*
> *We'll patient be and wait a bit.*"

Then she added: "I guess that we'll find plenty of field mice down on the Green Meadows when it is light, and we can catch them in the snow quite as easily as in the summer grass. Mrs. Grouse lives somewhere around here, and it may be that we can surprise her."

"Reddy's mouth watered at the thought, and as they sat there under the big hemlock tree, watching the first light of the morning creep through the Green Forest, Reddy thought more and more about Mrs. Grouse, until it seemed to him as if he could almost smell her, and that she must be very near. He was just going to say so to old Granny Fox, when a mass of snow was thrown right in his face, and with a great noise, something shot up so close to his nose that he almost fell over backward with fright.

"What — what was that?" he cried, when he could find his voice.

Granny Fox was grinding her teeth with rage. "That, you stupid, was the breakfast we ought to have had! That was Mrs. Grouse, and she was sleeping right under us all the time we have been sitting here!"

And from a safe place in a tall hemlock tree, Mrs. Grouse looked down and smiled on Granny and Reddy Fox.

"It's a nice snow, isn't it?" said she.

148